# NiGHT
# WiTCHES

# NiGHT WITCHES

## A NOVEL OF WORLD WAR II

Kathryn Lasky

Scholastic Inc.

Library of Congress Cataloging-in-Publication Data available

ISBN 978-1-338-15866-3

10 9 8 7 6 5 4 3 2 1    17 18 19 20 21

Printed in the U.S.A.    40
First printing 2017

Book design by Maeve Norton

# PART ONE

# CHAPTER 1

*"Noch' ved'm,"* I whisper to myself as I crouch in the rubble of our apartment building and watch the searchlights scraping the night, looking for those tiny planes, the U-2 trainers. Tatyana and I had both learned to fly these light biplanes, their four wings made of wood and canvas. Open cockpit. No parachutes. In these fragile machines the women of the 588th Regiment harass the German Sixth Army. The engines purr so softly that the Germans call them "sewing machines." But like small, sharp-beaked predatory birds, they will keep up the harassment until the dawn.

The Germans set up the searchlights to defend their fuel depots, ammunition dumps, ground troops, and support vehicles—all tactical targets for our Russian army. But that won't stop the *Noch' ved'm*, the Night Witches of the 588th Regiment, who weave through the sweeping beams of light in the loom of the Stalingrad night. The young women who attack Hitler's forces from the sky. My sister, Tatyana, is one of them. I might have been too, if I had lied about my age.

But Mama wouldn't let me lie. Although I'm only two years younger than Tatyana, my family has always treated me like I'm still a baby. They let Tatyana wear lipstick when she was twelve. But somehow, I was still "too young" at twelve. As for going downtown alone or with a friend, that wasn't allowed until this summer, and then the Germans came and wrecked everything.

Suddenly, there were Nazi soldiers on every street corner. They could stop you for no reason, and they loved to check young, pretty girls for weapons or cigarettes. It was not simply "frisking." *Groping* would be a better word. But then the heavy tanks rolled in, and the lewd glances of the soldiers were replaced by sniper fire and heavy bombs. The shelling has been constant ever since.

Mama is asleep now, beside me in this corner that we fashioned into a sleeping place. What was our living room is now strewn with bricks. One wall was blown out entirely two days ago. Three remaining walls still stand at right angles to one another. I stare at a calendar on one of the walls. How can a calendar be left? The bookshelves next to the calendar are in smithereens. Once, there were books all over our apartment, but now there are only fragments of pages that blow about like lost sheep scattered from their flock. For nearly two days I have tried to gather up some of these pages. It is a ridiculous task. If they aren't torn, they are scorched. I cannot imagine what I will do with them.

I spy another page, an illustration from *The Wonderful Wizard of Oz*. Glinda, the Good Witch of the South. She doesn't have a broom. No U-2 aircraft either. The good witch travels in a luminous peach-colored orb of light wearing a flowing gown. Not like our Night Witches in their flight helmets and goggles, with pistols tucked into their belts. Instead of wands, they have 175 kilos of bombs tucked under each wing.

As I bend over to retrieve the page with Glinda the Good Witch, I see my sister's broken sports trophies nearby. I could never really equal my sister as an athlete, but my parents didn't want me to feel bad, so they made up a certificate for me that read "Valya, you are the bright red star of our hearts." In a funny way, that certificate made it worse. I remember Tatyana's expression when they presented it to me at dinner that night. As Papa was making his little speech, there was a pitying smile on her face that said clear as any words that I would never be her equal, never quite catch up.

I love my sister, don't get me wrong. But her concern for me could be incredibly grating. Our biggest fight happened during the junior track meet when she tried to show me how she sailed over the hurdles. She had a particular way of jackknifing her knees up so she never grazed the boards. It worked for her, but not me. "It will," she said. "When you get a little bit taller. Maybe a centimeter."

"That's not the issue," I snapped. I was tall for my age, and already nearly her height. "It won't work. I am not a centimeter-smaller copy of you, no matter how badly everyone wants me to be."

In the next track meet, however, I did do well—very well. But no one paid one bit of attention to me. Why? Because in the event just before mine, the pole vault, Tatyana had broken the long-standing girls' record for our school. Hardly anyone was there to witness my accomplishment. They were all over on the field where the pole vaulting took place. My best friend, Irina, was sitting in the bleachers practically all by herself, clapping her hands violently and whooping her lungs out.

Tatyana had always outshone me in everything—except for flying.

My sister and I had both learned to fly by the time we were twelve years old. Our father was head of the flight training program at Engels airbase, not far from Stalingrad. I'd flown Yak trainers, U-2s, and several others. It was not that unusual, as flying clubs had become very popular between the two wars. We were just very lucky to have a father who was not only a seasoned pilot but a major in the Russian air force renowned for his skillful instruction. Some pilots are great flyers but not especially good teachers. Our father was a great flyer *and* a great teacher.

*   *   *

I notice that not only is the calendar intact, but the pencil is still suspended on a string beside it. From where I am crouched, I can see that Mama made a mark on the calendar two days ago. That was the day Grandmother, my babushka, was killed. Why would Mama do that? Was the mark for my grandmother? A tombstone made with a pencil?

She was killed by a roof timber that crashed when the Nazis dropped the bomb that took down the wall. Her head was smashed in on one side. And yet her face was remarkably unscathed. There was, however, a startled look in her eyes, as if she were asking "How could you do this to me?" Her limbs were all askew, like a marionette that had come loose from its strings. Her legs were broken in several places, and one leg from her knee down was bent back at a crazy angle. Somehow in the rubble, Mama found a lace-trimmed handkerchief and placed it over my grandmother's eyes, as if she didn't want Babushka to see the devastation of what had been her home for nearly thirty years. Then Mama bent over her with deep concentration and began to gently move her legs and arms, tending to this broken marionette. I made myself watch, pressing my hands against my mouth so I would not cry out loud. But Mama did not shed a tear. She just murmured softly to Babushka, as she had whispered to me when I had been a child with a high fever. "It's all right, Mama, Lena is here. You'll be right as rain tomorrow. Lena is here. Right as rain but the sun will shine."

Shortly after that the Germans seized our city. Like an invading herd of rabid beasts, the Nazi bombers turned the sky dark. First the Stukas—dive bombers—then the tanks. It was hard to believe even a mouse could have survived the bombardment, let alone human beings. The sound was so deafening for so long that Mama and I couldn't hear each other for several hours.

The sky is still brown from the dust and ashes of the bombing. Air-raid warning sirens rake our days and nights, along with the ceaseless bark of an urgent voice from our local Komsomol: "Air raid! Air raid!" But even the shelters have been bombed and our neighborhood cratered out so that the exposed cellars offer no protection at all.

A Komsomol unit comes routinely through our street to collect the bodies. They took Babushka away within hours. But they missed the horse in the pile of rubble with its legs sticking up in the air. Across the street from us, the entire block has been wiped out except for two buildings that lean shoulder to shoulder like two old cripples trying to prop each other up.

A few blocks down the street, a main sewer line has been bombed. Now the stench from a vast pool of sewage engulfs the neighborhood. It's hard for me to believe that just one month ago, the scent of cinnamon swirled through our apartment as Babushka's summer pudding cake baked in the oven.

Across the street from our apartment building, a wrecked

panzer tank is serving as a refuge for two families. I witnessed a fight earlier when relatives from one of their families arrived wanting to move in, but they were turned away.

A maple tree on the corner had just started to turn golden when, a few days ago, an explosion from a phosphorus bomb snagged it. The tree burst into flame—a pre-autumnal flare, precisely the color it would have been in another two weeks. Now it is a blackened corpse. It was the only tree on our block. Four months ago, I helped Mama plant pansies around its base. Mama believed that from every window in our apartment we should be able to see something lovely. But now the tree is gone. The object of our pride replaced by a new "pride"—the very unlovely Pak 38 antitank gun that our Red Army captured.

I turn the calendar back three pages to June 22. That was the day the unthinkable occurred. The Nazis invaded Russia. Operation Barbarossa, they called it. The largest invasion force ever assembled in Europe burst like a tidal wave across the Soviet border. The nonaggression pact Stalin had signed with Hitler was made obsolete within the space of one morning. Over seven hundred Russian aircraft were instantaneously destroyed while still on the ground. Then came the official announcement over loudspeakers blasting throughout the city from Commander Molotov, commissar of foreign affairs: "Men and women, citizens of the Soviet Union." His voice seemed to tremble. "At four a.m. and without declaration of war and without any claims being made on the Soviet Union, German troops attacked out country." We all froze. I can remember exactly where everyone was. Mama, Babushka, Tatyana, and I were all in the kitchen. Babushka was sitting reading a newspaper at the table with her magnifying glass. She recoiled suddenly, as though articles reporting Hitler's gains in Slovakia and Bulgaria had leapt into life in front of her very eyes. She looked toward the door as if expecting a jackbooted Nazi to burst in. Mama was standing up turning the tuning pegs of her violin. The D string was off. Tatyana was about to bite into a *vatrushka* bun. It was the season for those delicious cherry-filled pastries.

I was reading *Huckleberry Finn* for the third or fourth time. How I longed for his river! Our river, the Volga, was a wall the Nazis were pressing us up against. But that big, broad Mississippi was pure freedom. Huck says "in two seconds away we went a-sliding down the river, and it did seem so good to be free again and all by ourselves on the big river, and nobody to bother us."

How I wanted to slide away!

Molotov's voice continued, gaining strength as he spoke. "The government calls upon you, men and women citizens of the Soviet Union, to rally even more closely around the glorious Bolshevik Party, around the Soviet government and our great leader, Comrade Stalin. Our cause is just. The enemy will be crushed. Victory will be ours."

I remember looking at Tatyana, then shifting my eyes to Mama. A secret signal seemed to crackle between them, as it always did right before Papa left for an undisclosed location—an airbase, undoubtedly, since he was a major. None of them ever included me in those looks. I'm not sure if it was to protect me or because they assumed I was too young to understand.

Tatyana put down the bun, wiped her mouth, and reached for her pocketbook hanging on a peg. I got up to follow. Mama reached out and grabbed me.

"No, not you!" she cried.

I watched Tatyana head out. "Where is she going? The Komsomol?" I asked, referring to the student branch of the Communist Party.

Mama's face went pale. "Where is she going?" I repeated.

"To the People's Volunteers."

"The P-V?" I repeated, feeling a rush of excitement. "Then I'm going too. I'm also part of this war. I can fly. I don't have to sit on the ground doing nothing."

"No, you're not." Mama's fingers dug into my shoulder. "You're too young. You don't have the training yet."

"I scored higher than Tatyana on the Grade Three navigation test at Engels, and I was a year younger when I took it!"

"I don't care how high you scored. The only place you're going is to the *gastronom* with me."

"The *grocery store?*" I stared at her. "Mama, please. I can help. I'm a great pilot, you know I am. Papa said so. His commanding officer, General Akiva, said so."

"Let your sister fly. We have to eat."

The anger that had been bubbling up in my chest turned to ash. They didn't trust me. Didn't believe in me. The Germans might've turned our world upside down, but some things would never change.

We weren't the only ones who'd decided to go to the store. The streets were chaos, and when we got to the grocery store, the line was blocks long. By the time we got home, Tatyana had returned and left again. Babushka was still at the table, tears running down her face. She turned to us. "She's already left for training. She took her warmest jacket and I gave her my fur wrap," she said dully.

"Your fur wrap?" Mama repeated. "The one you wear to the opera?"

"Yes. I doubt I'll have use for it for quite a while. I told her to cut it up and line her boots. Winter will be here soon enough."

I looked down at the table. The half-eaten bun was still there, surrounded by crumbs. How could this all have happened so fast? In less time than it had taken me to eat my breakfast, my sister had gone off to war. Soon she'd be in the air, leaving me on the ground, as useless as a scattering of crumbs.

Since that day, I have yearned for so much. I yearn for Babushka and the scent of summer pudding. I yearn for pansies. I yearn for Irina, my best friend. But I think she's dead. She lived in the apartment building on Gorky Street that was destroyed. I'm not sure if I want to know if she's alive, because if she's dead, I can't keep imagining our future. Irina and I had plans. Not big or important plans. Just small, silly plans. We were going to go to the store near the park where she heard they sold nail polish. We'd talked about going with Irina's aunt, who worked at the state theater, to go see rehearsals. Irina hoped to be an actress. She always thought that perhaps a director would discover her, just like Lana Turner was discovered eating ice cream at something called a "soda fountain" when she was just sixteen years old. Not that we get to see many Hollywood movies. The Communist Party censors what is shown. We'd also been excited to go skating this winter. Irina and I both had new ice skates that we were eager to show off. There is a part of the Volga that freezes solid in January. Tea vendors and bakers sell food along the banks. Before last spring, we always had to go with our older sisters. Now we are finally allowed to skate on our own, and guess what happens? Our city is invaded by Nazis.

But of all the things I want to do, I yearn to fly the most. My father didn't just teach me how to read the instruments, he taught me how to fly beautifully, with skill and precision.

How to initiate not just a turn but a lovely, efficient turn that carves the sky like a bird's wings. How to "crab" for a cross-wind landing. How to catch an updraft from a warming earth.

To fly is to slip the cords of earth and join the sky. When you fly in an open cockpit like that of the U-2, you are wrapped in the wind. If you love a sunset, you become part of that sunset. You do not simply see the colors but feel them, as you feel the hush of the dawn steal into your soul when you fly east in the earliest hours of morning.

Mama stirs. "Do you think Tatyana is out there in all that?" she asks, and strokes my arm. The Nazis have surrounded three sides of our city with searchlights and flak guns. These are precisely the targets that my sister and her fellow pilots in their tiny planes want to bomb. Mama is looking out at the threads of red light from the antiaircraft emplacements that fracture the night and the screams of artillery shells as they seek their targets. Each evening the belly of the sky is ripped wide open and the glistening entrails of the night spill out in a slime of fire.

"Is she out there? Do you think so, Valya?" Mama asks again. She has her arm around my shoulder. I feel her fingers dig in, as if she is trying to hang on to me, the bright red star of her heart. But the other red star, the true red star, is out there in her tiny plane defending our city. I look up at the plumes of smoke rising from the bombed buildings.

"Maybe," I answer. "But dawn is coming. So not for long."

"You really wanted to go, didn't you?" she whispers hoarsely.

"It's all right, Mama." It's not all right, of course. But I can't tell Mama this now. She has lost so much: her own mother; my father, who is missing in action, maybe a prisoner of the Germans. Tatyana up there every night with a very good chance of dying. War is a time of giving up dreams, but it doesn't seem fair to me because my dream is to fight. To fly. Flying is the one thing I do as well as Tatyana. In school, she took firsts in math, firsts in literature and chemistry. But I passed every flight test with top marks. I was a so-so math student, but when I took the flight-training navigational tests I didn't make one mathematical error. When I was flying, everything came together for me.

I can't help but wonder what would have happened if we had gotten out of the city, across the river. But now there is no place else to go. We are pressed between the west bank of the river and the Nazis. It is said that they send one thousand planes a day to bomb us. It's enough to break not just a city but the entire sky.

"I know you could have flown as well as any of them," Mama says. "But, darling girl, it also takes maturity to fly in combat. That's why it is different for Tatyana. She is older. At her age she is more prepared to deal with the pressures of air combat."

The way Mama is talking, it sounds as if Tatyana is a thousand years old instead of eighteen.

"Perhaps if I took up the violin again, you'd encourage me to go fly," I say, trying to make a joke.

"You had an ear; you just didn't practice. You had as much potential as any one of my students."

"Not as much as Martina."

Mama reaches over and pats my hand. "Martina's arrogance will spoil her musicality. Just you wait and see."

*Wait and see?* As if we have all the time in the world.

"Do you think our violins survived?" Mama asks, then lets out a harsh laugh. "The violin survives so that the little Austrian corporal can fiddle on our graves like Nero." Mama and Papa always referred to Hitler as the little Austrian corporal. As a major in the air force, Papa enjoyed demoting him from führer to corporal.

I feel the grip of my mother's fingers relax as she begins to stroke my shoulder and hum a fragment of something. A Mozart violin concerto. There is a long, melodic, dreamy passage in the second movement that Mama loves and plays so beautifully in concert. Her fingers lift and press on my shoulder, as if she were playing her violin. I have become her strings, her fingerboard. Her voice is soft, like a zephyr in the flak-riddled night. I feel a harmony push from my throat and I join her, a whisper riding on the zephyr, and lean my head into the curve of her neck. The vibrations grow stronger as she approaches the cadenza.

Then the moment is over, and suddenly the sky bleeds light, followed by a sound so deafening that my guts rattle inside me. I gasp. It is as if the air has been sucked out of the city, out of me. Mama and I clutch each other. This is the end . . .

The end of us, but not the calendar. Half of another wall tumbles down. Yet the calendar still hangs from the other one on its peg. Is it still here to taunt us? Mama and I remain clutching each other. How long? I am not sure. Finally Mama gets up on her knees.

"Where are you going?" I ask, reaching for her.

"Do you hear a baby crying? I worry it might be Andrei. Poor Polina!" I do hear a faint wail scratching the air. I close my eyes and try not to imagine little Andrei crushed under piles of debris. Mama has never really cared for Andrei's mother, Polina. She thinks she is stingy and foul tempered, suspects her of hoarding, but is quick to excuse her, for after all, she has a baby to feed.

The cries fade, and Mama returns to huddle next to me. Perhaps half an hour passes before we dare move. Finally Mama whispers, "Do you think it's safe?" Then she gives me a withering look, as if to say "What is safe?" But at least we haven't heard any more bombs. Mama scrambles up from the floor toward the blown-out window. From where I crouch I can see Polina skittering like a crab over a pile of twisted iron and fragments of concrete.

"Polina, are you all right? How's the baby?" Mama leans far out the window and calls.

Those are her last words.

The crack of a rifle shot rips through the air. Mama slumps over the windowsill, then begins to fall through the window, clutching her throat. The air is shredded with the staccato barrage of rifle fire. I am mute. Paralyzed. My eyes widen but cannot see. *No. No. No.* The single word echoes throughout my body, shivers down my bones. The full realization of this moment creeps through me and spreads like a slow poison.

Mama is more than half out the window. Her knee appears hooked on the sill. There is still gunfire out there. I pull on her foot to bring her back in. Her shoe comes off in my hand, and then she falls the rest of the way out the window. I clutch her shoe to my chest. "Mama, Mama!" I whisper as I collapse on the ground.

I think of the calendar. It is September 2, a Wednesday. Should I make a mark for Mama as she did for Babushka? The cold ache of loneliness fills my body. The screams finally break through my skin. My bones clatter with fear, with fury, but mostly with grief. I think of Mama bending over her mother. So tenderly arranging Babushka's limbs, delicately putting the handkerchief over her eyes.

I am in a free fall through a terrible eternity. I feel my screams but cannot hear them. My babushka died two days ago. My father is missing. My sister is up there, but for all I know, she's been shot down. I am alone. I have been hollowed out like the buildings that stand around me. I am becoming a piece of dust, cosmic dust blown into the dark void of the forever. "Mama!" I whisper into the void. "Mama!" The words are swallowed into the nothingness.

# CHAPTER 2

When I finally fall asleep, curled on the floor splattered with my mother's blood, I dream of flying. I dream of the sky over the Sea of Azov, the shallowest sea in the world, and one of the most beautiful. We would go there for holidays, and as my father knew the director of the local flying club, we would fly half the day. Papa said it was the best place to train, for there was a peculiar magnetic anomaly that threw off the compass ever so slightly. Flying with a proper compass was easy, Papa said. But flying with one that has gone mentally cross-eyed is another thing entirely. In my dream I am no Night Witch. I am flying in the bright sunshine of summer. The glittering water of the sea is beneath me. There are the long stretches of beach that edge the water like a golden necklace. I skim low in the little biplane. In my dream I do the mathematics without even realizing it. The computations magically transmit to my hands on the control column and my feet on the rudder pedals.

I fly over the Kerch Strait. The Black Sea unfolds beneath me. The water is like liquid sapphires, and the reflections of clouds drift lazily across the surface. I fly low and so very slow. That is the beauty of the U-2 trainer. It can fly slower than the stall speed of any plane in the world. It is like walking through air.

I bank steeply and turn east. Dusk is settling across the land and over the steppes. A wonderful wild scent suffuses the air, for the steppes are in bloom. Tiny specks of color dot the long grasses. There is a sliver of moon that is magically growing fatter by seconds. By the time I am over the Sea of Azov it is full, and a pillar of moonlight stretches across the water. I see the shadow of my own wings printed against the moon. My wings are the smile in the moon's face. Then the sky flinches. There is a hideous flare of white. Once more the night is bleeding light, and I wake up, my heart racing.

There is no one to stop me now. No one to say I am too young — or at least not Mama. Not Papa. Not Babushka. I have lost everything, but I could join Tatyana in the sky. I could become a Night Witch. But how would I do it? Where would I go? Stalingrad is an island in this sea of war. We're surrounded by Nazis, backed up against the river—*trapped*. The 588th Regiment of Tatyana's has temporary airfields, but they are far outside the city. Hidden. There are no lights, nothing to reveal their location. I realize my idea is impractical, but it will not die. It begins as a little flicker but it quickly becomes a flame. I feel it burning within me. There *must* be a way.

I look around at the ruined walls of the apartment. There is nothing here for me. Just rubble. I am not sure how long I sit there thinking, but it has grown dark. My heart flies into my throat as I realize I'm not alone. There's a figure huddled by the calendar with a rifle aimed, not at me, but at what was once a window on Shkolnaya Street.

"Stay down," the figure hisses. There is the sharp crack of gunfire. I flinch and fall back. Then there's a second shot. I see the flash from the rifle. "Keep down."

The air rings with more shots. The acrid smell of gunfire hangs in the dimness. Then there is a long silence followed by a shout. It's a single word that I do not recognize, but it sounds slightly Turkic, the language of the people from the Ural Mountains. I can tell it was *not* German. For this I am thankful. The figure is now crawling toward me. Scraps of rifle smoke hang in the air.

"You all right?" he says in perfect Russian. I blink. It's Yuri, the boy often bullied in school. He was an easy target. Not only was he short, but his eyes tilted and he spoke with an accent. I must look completely stunned, because he doesn't look like a bully's target now. He has grown taller and his shoulders have broadened. His black hair slashes across his forehead. He looks dangerous.

"Yeah, it's me. Slit Eye. That's what they called me during sniper training. 'Hey, Slit Eye, you should be able to shoot.' Damn right, I say."

A dreadful feeling floods through me. "You didn't kill my mother, did you?"

It's as if his mouth tries to shape the words but they won't come out, so he shakes his head. I relax ever so slightly. "No, not me," he says finally. "When I got here I saw the Komsomol picking up a body from just outside your window there. That was your *mother*?"

"Yes."

Yuri sighs. "Alex and I had just arrived when they were taking her and some others away. We thought Otto might be holed up in that building across the way."

"Who's Otto?"

"Nazi sniper."

"You know his first name?" I ask incredulously.

"Of course. He's famous." Yuri gives me a small smile. "But not as famous as I'm going to be."

I remember hearing that Yuri's father had been a hunter in the Urals. He came from a long line of hunters, and Yuri claimed to hunt with a bow and arrow. He was always talking about the woods being filled with live animals. In winter he wore a fur hood from a wolverine he had shot. We were all city kids. He was not. He looked so different and his accent was so odd. I felt sorry for him, but of course I was scared to say the slightest thing to him, for befriending the target of bullies could make me vulnerable. I feel ashamed now.

Yuri shakes out a cigarette and lights it, cupping his

hand to shield the flame from a breeze. The orange glow illuminates his face. I am looking at a sniper, I remind myself. And all snipers are part of the secret police, the NKVD. The very abbreviation seems dark, lethal. It was the NKVD that organized the various militias in Stalingrad. They are always alert for deserters, counterspies, and the civilians who aid the Germans. In short, collaborators.

My friend Lara's father was hauled off in the middle of the night by the NKVD and never seen again. Suspicion is the NKVD's lifeblood. It pumps through their arteries from their darkest hearts. Two months ago the local NKVD came to our apartment building to organize the tenants for trench digging. No one refused. To refuse was to come under suspicion of being a collaborator. Not even Ekaterina Skolvich, who was close to ninety years old, refused.

But in addition to being alert for spies and collaborators, they have a keen eye for young people from the Komsomol who might make promising snipers. Just before school finished for the summer, we were all given eye tests. There was a rumor that students with exceptionally keen eyesight were being considered for a special marksmanship division in the NKVD, and Yuri, it was said, was one of those.

"Want one?" Yuri asks as he takes his first drag. It is a generous offer, as cigarettes have become very precious.

"No. I don't smoke. But thanks." The thanks sounds puny, as if I am trying to make up for what happened in secondary school. Does it count that I did not join in the bullying but merely stood by and watched?

"This has been going on for two days," he says.

I'm confused. "What, the war? The bombing?"

"No, the duel."

"What duel?"

"Alex and me and the Nazi sniper, Otto."

"You've been chasing one another for two days?"

"This would have been our third night. But the Nazi fell for the oldest trick in the book. Alex raised his helmet on a stick just a bit above that pile of rubble across the way. Otto shot at it and the bullet ripped the helmet apart." It seems strange to me that Yuri was on a first-name basis with the man he was trying to kill. "Then Otto reached up to retrieve his cartridge cases. The Nazis always do that after what they consider a successful shot. As Otto did. So I saw just a tiny wedge of his scalp. That was all I needed, a few centimeters. That did it."

"A few centimeters?" I reply, both impressed and horrified.

"I told you I am a good shot. Old Slit Eye!" He winks at me.

"Did Otto know *your* name? Are you that famous?"

Yuri actually blushes, levels his hand, and waves it back and forth. "Maybe just a little bit. I'm getting there."

It is quiet outside now. No sniper fire, no Stukas screaming across the night, but through the silence I hear the distinctive purr of a U-2.

"It's a Night Witch," Yuri says, and cocks his head toward the sky.

"I need to be there."

"Where? Where do you need to be?"

"Up there." I tip my head. "In the sky, with them. With the witches and my sister."

# CHAPTER 3

Yuri and I talk far into the night, each of us propped against our own broken wall. The first night I ever spend with a young man. I tell him about my dream of flying and how I want to join my sister, who's a Night Witch in the 588th Regiment.

"It'd be difficult to get out of Stalingrad," Yuri says. "And even more difficult to find the Night Witches' airfields. They move them all the time."

"I know, I know. It seems impossible."

"I don't believe in impossible."

"You don't?" I almost smile. It'd been nice to lose myself in this talk of flying. It felt so good to tell someone of my dream after avoiding it for so long with Mama. But then something shrivels inside me as Mama's face looms up. I'll never see her again. This too seems impossible. I'll never hear her voice, or her objections to me flying. I almost yearn for those objections just so I can hear her speak one more time.

I look out the window, or what was a window and is now a fragment of a wall with a huge opening. I am not sure how many hours have passed, but it looks as if the dawn is breaking, and it is beautiful. How can that be? How can the morning after my mother's death dare to dawn with this lovely glow in the eastern sky? How does this sun dare to rise? I look grimly out the opening and want to spit at the dawn.

"You thinking of your mother?" Yuri asks.

I nod. "My mother, and how I want to get out of this city. I want to fly."

"You know, Hitler has ordered the city cleared."

*Hitler?* Yuri speaks as if he is right here in Stalingrad. "What do you mean?"

"I mean the Nazis will order civilians out of the city and march them to a camp."

My eyes dart around the ruins of our apartment. "Then we're trapped," I say.

"It's true. There's nowhere to run between here and the Volga."

"I'd sooner drown." He says nothing. "Someone says the Nazis have killed forty thousand Russians every day since they reached the city. Is that true?" I ask.

"I don't know how many are left. I don't keep count of how many General Paulus and his Sixth Army kill. I just keep track of my own kills. Which reminds me, do you have a pencil? I lost mine."

"There was one around here once. Look on the floor. It might still be there." I point toward the calendar, and he crawls over to it. Despite his heavy boots, he makes no noise at all. He could have been a ballet dancer but instead he's a sniper.

"Ah, here it is!" His narrow eyes glitter with triumph. I wonder if they look the same way when he kills someone.

He takes out a tiny piece of paper stuffed in a pocket and makes a mark. I am tempted to ask how many this makes but stop myself. If he's proud of his accomplishments, I don't want to know. Although it strikes me that he does not seem like a proud person, despite his comment about the Nazi sniper possibly knowing his first name.

Yuri makes the mark, stuffs the paper back in his pocket, then looks up at me. "There might be an alternative."

"Alternative to what?"

"Alternative to a forced march to a Nazi internment camp. There's a rumor of another planned evacuation to the east bank of the river. It'll be huge, though. You need to get down there early. Go now if you can."

"Now? Before an order is given?"

A fierce light burns in his eyes. "You know what the commander of the Russian Sixty-Second Army says, don't you?" I shake my head. How would I know what General Vasily Chuikov says? "Chuikov says every person is his own general in this battle for Stalingrad. You should go before it is too late. No waiting around for orders, or else the next person who might be giving them to you could be Adolf Hitler." He pauses. "You know the witches destroyed one of the big searchlights the other night?"

"Really?" Maybe it was Tatyana who shot it out. I can imagine her zeroing in on a target, chewing her lip. That was an odd habit of hers. I wonder if after this war she'll even have lips.

If she were flying, her hand would be steady on the control stick, her voice crisp as she asked her navigator for her bearings. I know she would be calm. I suppose this is what Mama meant when she spoke about the pressure of air combat. But I too have great powers of concentration. I live in a city that's been under constant bombardment for weeks. One shores up their house as best they can. You find what food you can. You take care of your dead as best you can.

What Yuri says about leaving early, about how everyone is their own general, excites me. Maybe if I can get on this transport to the east bank, I'll somehow find a temporary airfield, maybe the one with Tatyana. She'll tell them how well I fly. She'll tell them that I passed the navigation test with scores higher than hers!

I turn to Yuri. "Maybe it's my sister who shot out the big searchlight."

"That would make her very brave. Braver than any sniper." He pauses a long time. "Look, Valentina."

"You know my name?" I don't know why I am so startled, as we have now spent several hours together. But this is the first time he has addressed me by name.

"Yes. Why does that surprise you?"

"It just does." I smile grimly. "I am not a famous sniper."

"I know your name because when kids bullied me in school, you would rush by and not look. I could see that you were ashamed. Ashamed of them."

"I am ashamed of myself. I did nothing to stop it."

"That's not important. You did not take part in it. Some kids just did it because their friends did. But listen to me. This isn't school. The Nazis are not mere schoolyard bullies. Go . . . go now. This city will be an ocean of flames in another week. It's bloody and will get bloodier."

"But where should I go?"

"Go wait for the steamer. Get as close to the river as you can, close to where the troop and supply-ferry jetties are. Soon, before the sun fully rises. You'll be a difficult target." He has taken off the knapsack and, cracking the magazine of his rifle open, begins to shove cartridges in. He moves and braces himself against the edge of the blown-out window. "Climb out here and run. I'll cover you. Though it seems quiet now."

I look at him. *You'll cover me*, I think. *And if I get shot by a Nazi sniper you'll use my body for a barricade?* I know that the Red Army soldiers often use bodies as barricades. The tops of trenches are stacked with bodies—bodies and sandbags. "Go, Valya."

I am shaking so hard I think I hear my own teeth chattering. "I don't think I can do it. I'm too scared."

"You'd be crazy if you weren't scared. Just go. Please!"

I look at him once more before I go. "Thank you, Yuri Yurovich Vaznov."

"You know my full name, my father's name?"

"Yes. I saw it on the attendance list in Grosnov's math class." I swing my leg over the remnants of what had been a windowsill, over the bloodstains from my mother's torn throat, and dash into the empty street.

I don't look back. There's no looking back. But I can't help wondering if I'll ever see Yuri again. Yuri, the boy who knew my name and whose name I never spoke aloud until last night.

As I slip from the window into the early dawn studded with flashes of gunfire, I cannot help but think of another window from my childhood, a window far, far away from here, in London. This home was occupied by a family named Darling. They had three children: Wendy, John, and Michael. One cold winter night, the nursery window blew open, and a boy named Peter flew through it to search for his lost shadow. He was accompanied by his fairy companion, Tinker Bell. Peter enchanted the three children with his tales of Neverland. He quickly taught them to fly and they all flew out the window, then set a course for the second star to the right and straight on till morning.

Now, as I tear through the city, there is no tinkling of bells, no fairy language, just gunfire. I see my shadow sprinting across rubble. Shall I lose my shadow like Peter Pan? It stretches out ahead of me as I leap over a body dressed in camouflage. The head is still in the split helmet. So this is the other duelist. *Otto, the Nazi sniper,* I think as I sail through the air like a broad jumper. The sound of panzer fire and heavy artillery gnashes the dark. Second star to the right? If only I could fly.

# CHAPTER 4

It takes me ages to get through the maze of streets as I make my way to the waterfront. Many of the streets are clogged with tank units. Others are engulfed with flames. But I have to get to the waterfront. I have to get on that steamer and out of the city. Then I'll somehow figure out where the airfields are. They're outside of Stalingrad, and I doubt they could be more than fifty kilometers. After all, the fuel load on the biplanes is limited. They can't fly too far from their base. I'll find them. I will. I smile to myself. Like Yuri, I've stopped believing in impossible.

I finally arrive on Gvardeyskaya Street, a short distance from the jetties. It is being heavily bombarded from both sides. The German Stukas screech horribly overhead, their black tails with the broken crosses cutting against the pink dawn. Like schooling sharks, their shadows mass over the city. The east side of the Volga River has become a huge Red Army mustering ground for men, supplies, and the batteries of the latest weapon, the Katyusha rocket launcher. It's named for a popular, romantic wartime song, but when the rockets are launched, there is a deathly scream.

But the German Sixth Army is not to be deterred so easily, and they keep pouring their own bombs and rockets into the city. I hop between the trenches that the neighborhood militias have built, the top edges stacked with sandbags and dead bodies, and race down an alley that gives me a clear view of the railroad station. I catch a blurred glimpse of the famous dancing-children statue. They are still frozen in their joyful dance around the crocodile—taunting it, I suppose. No one has ever really explained the story to me. Something about a crocodile who was coaxed into devouring a pirate. But now the crocodile has come right into our city. And yet these children cast in metal still dance while I run for my life.

I'm dashing down the street when something pulls me literally off my feet, down into the trench.

"Comrade Baskova!"

"Anna!" I cry as my eyes fall on the familiar face of my classmate. She played water polo for our local team and was high-ranking in the school division of the Komsomol.

"Come with me. We need you for a gun crew."

I wonder who *we* is. Her neighborhood Komsomol unit? Or is she in a unit of the NKVD? If so, I need to be careful. I can hear people crawling around in the trench, which seems to be several hundred meters long.

"I can't," I say, shouting to be heard over the gunfire. "I'm heading to the docks. I need to get on the ferry. I have to find . . ." I trail off as Anna pushes me along the trench to an area where it widens to make room for two antiaircraft guns with their barrels resting over the embankment. Six young people are manning them.

"I can't do this," I repeat. "I know nothing about guns."

"You'll learn. Mikhail, show Comrade Baskova how it works."

A boy no older than twelve comes up to me. He is wearing an *ushanka* earflap hat with a red star on the front, but the rest of his clothes are ragtag remnants. His face is grimy and he smells of smoke. He begins speaking with a weary voice that does not match his youthful appearance. "This is an M1939, a 37-millimeter antiaircraft gun. The largest antiaircraft gun we use in Trench 301." I stare at him, uncomprehending. Not one of the people in the trench is in the Red Army. Most aren't even old enough. Yet here they are, operating deadly weapons.

Mikhail continues. "This side wheel controls the elevation. We have just switched targets from the Stuka bombers over the city to the panzers. Look at them out there!" He points over the trench. In the distance, I can see three tanks advancing. "Like they're going for a Sunday stroll, eh? Watch this." He presses his eye against a scope, turns a wheel that lowers the elevation of the barrel, then fires. A moment later, the tank is blown to smithereens. I hear Anna give a whoop.

"No more walk in the park," Mikhail says. "Watch me. See, you turn this wheel to lower or raise the barrel."

This is all happening too quickly. My chest fills with anxiety that has nothing to do with the gunfire. "I can't stay here. I need to get to the docks."

"What?" Anna snaps. "What's important? What's more important than this battle?"

"I'm getting out. On that ferry. I'm joining the Night Witches."

"Don't be ridiculous!" Anna scoffs while Mikhail's eyes dart back and forth between us. If indeed they are NKVD, they could shoot me right here for desertion, or for being a traitor. A *coward*. But I'm not a coward. I want to fight. I want to fly!

"My sister is a Night Witch. I also fly, and I'm going to join her." I cringe as I hear how stupid this sounds. But I shove my doubts aside. I don't care what other people think. I'm going.

A look of disgust sweeps across Anna's face. "You know I can report you to the NKVD for refusing to serve."

"You wouldn't," I say, glaring at her. She was a *hall monitor*, and now she's threatening to report me to the NKVD?

"I would. Then they'll shoot you as a collaborator." Her eyes are like ice.

I shut my own eyes for a moment as I envision hundreds of thousands of German troops—a virtual sea of Germans—between me and Tatyana. What choice is there but to join in and begin killing them one at a time? "All right," I say quietly. I'll get out of here eventually. I'm not sure exactly how. But I'll do it. I'm not spending the rest of the war in a trench.

"Up two degrees, left one degree," Mikhail barks. He's standing on a step, but it's not quite high enough. He still has to stand on tiptoe in order to press his eye to the scope. But his aim is excellent. When his left foot strikes the fire pedal, he always hits his target, bringing the lumbering panzers to their knees like huge prehistoric behemoths. Men, or pieces of men, go flying. Mikhail remains unfazed, an unlit cigarette clamped in the corner of his mouth.

I do the best I can, taking orders as I try to wrap my head around the surreal situation. After four hours we are given a break. A new crew comes in and we crawl down the trench to the "lounge." A euphemistic name for a part of the trench that's a little wider. The ceiling is somewhat higher, so we sit on old ammo crates. There is a picture of Mickey Mouse wearing an *ushanka* specially cut for his big ears. On another wall there is a dartboard with a picture of Adolf Hitler. In the center of the room is a "table" made from a box that's covered with a flowered cloth. There's a candle shoved in an empty vodka bottle. The homey touch is wasted on me, however. I just want to be in a cockpit and not stuck underground with candlelight and a steady supply of vodka.

Mikhail lights up the cigarette and offers me one.

"No, thanks."

Anna arrives carrying a bottle of vodka and three metal cups. It is the cheap kind, the kind that my father never drank. Anna pours a minuscule amount into a cup and hands it to me. "We operate under the same rules as the Red Army. One hundred grams of food a day. Plus I managed a bit of sausage." She draws out her knife, and just as she does, a rat suddenly appears and grabs one end of the sausage. Anna lunges at the thief and comes back with both the rat and the sausage impaled on the blade. *"Na Zdorov'e!"* Anna and Mikhail both cheer.

She scrapes off the rat and the sausage. There is, of course, blood on the sausage. Anna opens the bottle of vodka again and pours a bit out to wash it off. "A gram or two for our friend. May your blood be cleansed with our good Russian vodka." She looks at the label. "Well, second-rate vodka." She laughs and the others join in. But I am too numb to laugh. In the span of a few hours, the dreams that had buoyed my spirits this morning seem to be slipping from my grasp.

"Hear! Hear! As it says"—Anna points the cup toward the words carved in the trench wall—"NOT ONE STEP BACK." That was the order direct from the Kremlin when the Nazis first reached the Volga. It became officially Order No. 227, designed to destroy retreat mentality. Order No. 227 stated that "panic-mongers and cowards" were to be destroyed on the spot, and that anyone who surrendered was a traitor to the Motherland. So that is what we drink to. The vodka burns as it goes down my throat. I keep my eyes locked on the words inscribed on the wall. Not One Step Back. *God give me the courage,* I think. *One Nazi at a time.* Somehow I'll get out of here. I refuse to spend the war underground, tethered to a machine gun.

By my next shift I have learned quite a bit about this group in Trench 301. They are mostly young women, girls like Anna. A large number of them are part of an antiaircraft regiment that distinguished itself in the defense of a tractor factory two weeks ago. They were brought into the city to fight in the trenches my mother and I dug in early August as part of the neighborhood militia.

They are making a difference. I have seen it in the short time I've been here. The Germans' panzer line has pulled back. I convince myself this is just a slight detour, that soon I will be on my way to join my sister and the Night Witches.

Under the leadership of our small commander, I learn how to work the gun, how to love the sound of a good hit, the thrill of the fragments of a tank exploding into the air. I am no longer crouched in the remains of our apartment building, cowering from the bombs. I am crouching in Trench 301 behind an antiaircraft gun, and my sister is in the air over Stalingrad in her U-2. We are both mastering the implements of war and Nazis are dying.

It is getting dark again. Anna crawls into the lounge and announces that there is ice on the river, "just a thin skim of it."

Mikhail mutters a curse word I've never heard a child say. "It's bad if the ferries can't get through."

"It's bad for the Nazis too," Anna says. "They don't have winter gear. Oh, that reminds me." She pulls out a *ushanka* earflap hat from her jacket and hands it to me.

"Where'd you get that?" Mikhail asks.

"From a fellow near the old clock factory. He won't be needing it anymore." She delivers this news placidly. I adjust the chin strap of the dead man's hat. It's strange to think that this strap pressed against the skin of someone who was alive hours ago. It's hard for me to believe that less than a year ago, my main concern in life was being able to go skating with Irina without our older sisters. War changes everything. War was never supposed to come this close.

I wonder what Tatyana would think if she knew I was wearing a dead man's hat. I know it doesn't make me more grown-up, really, but it means I have been close to danger. If she saw me in this hat stained with the blood of a Red Army lieutenant, she wouldn't tease me. She would not treat me as a baby. I'm a soldier. Not just her little sister.

Anna is still talking about the man who wore it.

"It belonged to Comrade Lieutenant Vladimir Dudonov. He was killed in a mortar attack near a German fuel depot. The Night Witches are out there raising hell. Look south. See that huge burning in the sky?"

"Yeah?" Mikhail says as I nod.

"That's the biggest Nazi fuel depot. They hit it an hour ago."

*Just an hour ago*, I think—not hours ago. One hour ago this hat was on Comrade Dudonov's head. How long will it last on my head?

Mikhail begins to wonder aloud. "I don't know how they do it. How those Night Witches sneak up so quiet on a target like the fuel depot."

"The U-2s are equipped with noise and flare mufflers. So they can approach undetected," I say. Both Mikhail and Anna look at me with surprise.

"How do you know all this?" Anna asks.

"I told you. I'm a pilot. And I'm going to be a Night Witch."

Anna raises an eyebrow and snickers. "I think I poured you too much vodka."

I feel rage kindling in me, just as it used to when Tatyana toyed with me. But Mikhail and Anna are not my siblings. They have no idea of my skills, capabilities. So I quell the rage and look at them steadily. My voice is even, almost toneless. "You thought I made that up about joining the 588th? I didn't. I know how to fly. I was in the aero club. My father is a major in the air force. I learned to fly in a U-2. They were our training aircraft."

"Look, there's one now!" Mikhail points to where we blasted the last panzer.

"There's two," I say. "No, actually, three . . . see the other ones?"

"They're flying right through the Nazi defense lines," Anna gasps. "And the searchlights have pinpointed them!"

Two of the U-2s peel off and a Messerschmitt 109 starts to give chase to the third plane. I watch breathlessly, and can almost feel the stick in my hands as I pull it sideways to slide off from the trace bullets. *Slow. Slow. Cut the speed to ninety kilometers,* I silently coach the pilot. She's doing it! The pilot is easing back on the acceleration until the little plane is flying way beneath the stall speed of the Messerschmitt that overshot her. Meanwhile the other two U-2s release their bombs. Seconds later another target is hit. The tortoise wins again and the hare is helpless. "Holy mother!" Anna whispers. "They got another big ammunition dump. Glorious!"

The three planes head in a new direction, and I can tell they're scrambling to switch positions. They take turns decoying the Nazis as they dive, slide, and slip through the latticework of the searchlights' beams that slice the blackness of the night. Then one flies off directly into the killing light to attract the enemy. It's a bold, taunting move—*Hey, hey, you can't catch me!* So the enemy gives chase while the other two Night Witches drill in on the target and release their bombloads.

It is relentless. It seems as if every three or four minutes new witches fly out into the night. I could do this. I know it. It's as if I'm up there in the cockpit. I feel that stick in my hand. I smell the sizzle of the tracer bullets. *That's* where I belong: up in the sky, not in this trench turning the wheel of this gun. I feel like I'm beating on the windows of the sky. *Let me in, let me in!* I am Wendy trying to crash into Neverland. *Let me in! Let me in!*

"No wonder they say the Germans are getting no sleep," Mikhail says.

"But how do they do it? How do they sneak up through all the flames, the fire, the tracer bullets?" Anna asks.

I'm not sure if she's referring to logistics or to courage, so I answer, "It's a decoy strategy. Three planes set out. One peels off and begins to fly crazily to get the attention of the enemy while the other two close in on the target. They both approach from a high elevation, then throttle back the engine to idle and slide into a steep dive, then fly low and drop the bomb before the enemy on the ground knows what's happening."

"So they fly with no lights?" Anna asks.

"None."

"What about parachutes?" Mikhail asks.

I shake my head. "No, nothing. It's an open cockpit, all fabric and wood. There's a compass and a navigator in the rear with a map but no radio. A five-cylinder radial engine with one hundred horsepower. Bomb racks and a light machine gun sometimes. That's about it. But that means the stall speed of the aircraft is half that of a fighter plane, and the German fighter plane can't fly slow enough to stay with them." My voice grows softer and softer, until it seems as if I am talking to myself. I am in a kind of waking dream.

Anna leans forward. Her face is large, with somewhat indistinct features that seem to blend into each other. "You know all this from being in an aero club? Even though there was no war to fight then?"

"I wasn't in a war, but I can still see the Night Witches' strategy. The planes are perfect for this. They can fly slow, slower than the Stukas. It's the old story."

"What old story?"

"The tortoise and the hare."

"No!" Mikhail gasps suddenly. His eyes widen in horror at something outside the trench. We follow his gaze.

High up, caught in the web of the searchlights, a U-2 is burning. It seems as flimsy as a paper kite, or a moth that has flown too close to a flame. It will be ashes in seconds, but I can see parts of the fuselage falling, the wings and the tail drifting slowly to the ground. Could it be Tatyana? Something hardens in me. I want to stop these monsters.

I turn abruptly to Anna. "Comrade Anna, I'll be more helpful up there than down here. I just know it."

"You are saying that now, after what you just saw?" Anna asks. I nod. "You're crazy! A complete lunatic!" But I can see she's suppressing a smile. A smile, not a smirk like the one Tatyana sometimes gave me. She starts to leave, then turns around, her face suddenly serious. "There is a rumor that the NKVD will allow civilians to cross the river tomorrow. They have a steamship ready." So Yuri was right. There will be an evacuation. Anna leans forward. "If you are as good a flyer as you say, maybe you can get to an airfield somehow. But get to the jetty early. They are supposed to board at dawn. You have a few hours." I start to stand up.

"For God's sake, don't forget your hat." Mikhail stands and plops the *ushanka* on my head. I can only hope I do better than the man who wore it.

# CHAPTER 5

The streets near the jetty are packed with crowds. There are thousands of people, and I'm still two blocks from the river. Everyone's jostling, trying to get as close to the river as possible. There's a mother with a wailing baby whose mouth is stretched into an enormous black hole emitting screams. I see another child, no more than eight, with a toddler tied to his back. The toddler seems almost as big as the child. A fierce, toothless old lady swings her cane while casting vile curses at everyone in her way.

I bump into something.

"I beg your pardon!" The voice is angry.

"I'm sorry . . . Martina!" I stare in shock at my mother's best violin student, standing there clutching her violin case. Her violin case!

"You of all people should understand," she snaps.

"Understand what?"

"The value of what I am holding in my arms." Her stupid violin has survived. Yes, it is an expensive one. Not a

Stradivarius but a Viktor Marakova, who had been an apprentice to the czar's violin maker, Nicolaus Ferder Kittel.

"What does that matter now?"

"What does it matter? How can you ask such a question?"

"Your teacher is dead," I reply. "Maybe you'll find a new one."

She scowls. "What are you talking about?"

"My mother, your teacher, is . . ." But at that moment there is a surge in the crowd and we are all pushed forward. Like an undertow, it threatens to pull me down. My feet leave the ground for several seconds as the mob pushes. But then somehow, miraculously, I make it to the jetty. The gangplank for the steamer has been lowered, and Martina is once again next to me with her stupid violin, which she is now holding above her head. She is snarling at everyone around her. A man shoves me, and I fall to the ground, crying out as boots stomp all over me. Someone has me by the collar and is pulling me. I can only hope they are dragging me toward the steamer.

They are not. I am sitting on the rubble of what had been a broad sidewalk, blood running from my nose. Across the way I see people boarding the steamer. I try to get up and a hand pushes me back down.

"No!" a voice barks. I look up. The dark eyes look down at me grimly.

"Yuri! What are you doing here?" His hand presses hard on my shoulder and I try to fling it off. "I want to go. Let me go." He slings an arm around my chest and drags me back even farther. "Let me go! What are you doing? I . . . I . . . don't understand . . ."

"The steamer can't handle all those people. It will sink or tip over. It's insane," he snaps.

I can't believe that he stopped me. Fury builds inside me as I try to wrench myself free, but then Yuri looks at me with a mixture of tenderness and concern that makes me pause. "Here, let me help you," he says. "Your face is a bloody mess, and in this weather that blood will freeze."

He takes a kerchief from his pocket and hands it to me, but keeps his other hand on my shoulder. I just hold the kerchief. He takes it back from me and, holding my chin, begins to dab at my face. I don't feel pain. I don't feel blood. I just feel left behind. His hands are gentle, I think, for a sniper. His trigger finger dabs very delicately. "So much blood from such a small nose," he whispers. "But I think it's slowing down now."

I stand up slowly and watch the ferry pull away from the jetty. "What gives you the right to stop me? How can you have the nerve? You're the one who *told* me about the evacuation."

"I know I told you, but I had no idea it would be like this. So many people. I thought there would be more steamers. Bigger ones."

The boat moves through the water, carrying my hopes along with it. When it reaches the main stream of the river, it slows a bit as it encounters the current, but in a short time it will be on the east side. Although it's only a few kilometers away from Stalingrad, it might as well be light-years. My only chance is slipping away. My only chance to shatter that windowpane between me and Neverland is gone.

I hear Yuri inhale sharply as a gull-winged Stuka swoops down, the broken cross clearly visible on its tail. A fireball explodes in the air as the steamer bursts into flame. Ablaze, it lists to one side and then begins to sink. An eerie hush settles on the throngs of people still on the jetty. People who'd despaired at being left behind are now transfixed by the scene of certain death occurring before their eyes.

Trembling uncontrollably, I sink to my knees. *That could have been me*, I think, and then, *That is Martina!* Martina and her violin. That is the mother with her baby. That is the schoolboy with the toddler. That is the cursing old lady waving her cane.

When I turn to look for Yuri, he is gone. Gone to kill with his gentle sniper fingers that wiped the blood from my face. I look up at the sky. It is daylight. The witches sleep, and I am no closer to their airfields than I was before.

I turn and begin to thread my way back to Trench 301.

# CHAPTER 6

The weeks that follow are formless except for the fact that the weather is growing colder. Getting out of the city is impossible now. More German troops pour in. We blow them up, destroy their tanks, but they seem to multiply. I think of my biology class's regeneration experiments with the flatworms. We would cut them up and then they would regenerate the lost part—the head, the tail, sometimes within a day. We've got Nazi flatworms here.

Sometimes the sky is black with Stukas. The noose is tightening around my city. We crouch in our trench but the bombardment is endless. It seems like just a matter of time before an explosion finally rips us from the trench.

I think about Yuri. His fingers touching my face. His intense eyes peering through the crosshairs of his rifle. I try to banish him from my thoughts, reminding myself that he's a sniper. Snipers don't flirt.

Martina's face slides into my mind. The sneer curling across her face as she clutched her violin. I do not exactly grieve for her, but I have thought a lot about her, more specifically about her violin. Did it somehow survive, like the calendar hanging on the wall of our apartment? Is it floating down the river toward the Caspian Sea? It's growing colder, and the river might soon be locked in thick ice.

Could the ice be my blessing in some way? Could I walk across to the east side of the river and make it to the airbase at Akhtuba?

Two nurses from the civilian militia arrive to deliver some winter clothing, most of it taken off dead soldiers. They hand me bloodstained fur trousers, which I put on quickly, grateful for the warmth. The knee is shot out of one leg, and I assume that the soldier died during an attempted amputation. What does one call these clothes—hand-me-downs? *Not exactly*, I think. It's hardly as if they outgrew them.

We barely sleep except in small snatches when we are not operating the guns. I have not had a bath since before Mama died. Where would one bathe in a trench? Tatyana and I used to argue over who got the first bath when there was plenty of hot water. Now there is no water. We used to play games while we hung the laundry. Now there is no laundry and no make-believe.

Tatyana was always the boss in make-believe. We constantly fought for the role of Glinda the Good Witch.

"You can be a Munchkin," Tatyana would say. "They're so cute."

"No, they aren't. They're weird."

"Well, then, you can be the Wicked Witch of the East," Tatyana would reply calmly.

"And get squashed by Dorothy's house? Oh yeah. That's great, Tatyana."

Now Tatyana is a witch and I'm crammed in this trench and might as well be a Munchkin. And it's not make-believe and it's not Oz. It's Stalingrad and it's war.

Our lives revolve around these guns, around killing. I start to look forward to the visitors, who are a welcome distraction. One of my favorites is a Kazan Tatar, a cook from a Red Army antitank detachment. We call him Gunga Din because, like the legendary character in the Rudyard Kipling poem, he comes bearing water in the large Red Army thermoses. He also brings tea and soups, and crawls with these containers strapped to his back up to the front lines.

Yelena we call "the butcher." She is a mortar operator down the trench line from us, but when she is not manning the mortar, she creeps out with her knives and cuts meat off the dead horses.

I can't resist asking each visitor about the state of the river. How solid has the ice become? Yelena looks at me, her eyes full of warning. "Solid enough for a rocket launcher from the east bank to fall short and crack the river, taking five good citizens of Stalingrad walking across to the bottom of the river. So don't even think of it."

One day we hear that the central rail station has been taken by the Germans and the next day that Chuikov and the Red Army have taken it back. But the tide is beginning to turn ever so slightly. Soon, the word *kessel* is on everyone's lips—*kessel* or cauldron, like a witch's cauldron. The plan for Operation Uranus is to send our troops to surround the German Sixth Army, in a formation that mimics a cauldron. And then that cauldron is going to be turned upside down right on top of the Germans.

But the Germans are still obsessed with capturing Stalingrad. There's a rumor that the führer ordered that Stalingrad be captured by October 15. Yet October 15 comes and goes. By this time, I have learned not only the mysteries of the 37-millimeter antiaircraft gun, but I have become an efficient loader for the DP-28 machine gun. It's relatively light: eight kilos, or about twenty violins. Violins weigh about 400 grams. So I am now playing a DP-28 machine gun. A staccato nocturne.

My last conversation with Mama streams through my head. *Your father said you were a natural.*

*Better flyer than violinist.*

*You had an ear; you just didn't practice. You had as much potential as any one of my students.*

*Look at me play now, Mama,* I think as I finish loading the pan. Gregory is the operator of this gun. A tall, gangly lad of thirteen. He is very proficient. I have completed the loading but he is not firing.

"Something wrong, Gregory?" I shout as the din of gunfire reaches a deafening level. I look up and a fountain of blood pours down on me. Gregory begins to fall, his frozen eyes wide in disbelief. There is a hole in his forehead—a sniper bullet? The ground begins to rumble as a panzer rolls toward us, meters away. The machine gun is mounted on a tripod. I jump up and press my eye to the scope. I see the sniper. There is no pistol grip, just a trigger ring that I clutch, then pull. "Gregory," someone yells. "Get on the 37."

Where's Mikhail? Why isn't Mikhail on 37, our name for the antiaircraft gun? But there is no time to think. I run down the trench to Mikhail's station. He's been shot too. My little commander is bleeding. Bleeding but furious. "You have to do it, Valya. I can't." To my horror, I see he has a wrist that ends in a bloody mass—no hand.

"Do it, Valya. It's got a fresh belt in it. Do it!"

And so I do it. Once again I press my eye to the scope. The panzer is advancing. This will be the end of all of us. I turn the wheel. I get the panzer directly in the crosshairs and press the pedal. An enormous explosion rocks the trench, and I feel the rumble in my bones.

"You got it!" Mikhail cries, jubilation in his voice. I tear off my *ushanka* and wrap it around his bleeding stump.

"Mikhail," I whisper. "You can't die. You can't." Such a small boy and so much blood.

Anna rushes over to us. "What's going on? I saw Mikhail blow up one of the new super panzers just now." But stares at us, confused, unable to comprehend the scene before her.

"Valya blew it up. Not me."

"Valya?" she repeats numbly.

"Anna, we have to get him help. Is there a medic somewhere down the trench line?"

"I think so." Her eyes are glazed. She seems rooted to the ground.

"Go!" I scream.

The *ushanka* is now thoroughly soaked in blood. Mikhail is trying to talk, but his words are faint and slurred.

"Mikhail, don't talk. You need your energy. Please, hold on until the medic comes."

He has a faint smile on his face. He looks so young. Not the little old man anymore. "I want to tell you one thing."

I sigh and shake my head. What could he want to tell me that's so important? "What is that?" I say softly.

"I won't be able to play the piano anymore . . . You know I was fit for more than just firing the 37. I was accepted by the Gnessin Institute to study . . . to study with Evgenia Fabianovna herself . . . I don't want to brag, but they said I was a prodigy."

I bend over close to his face and whisper into his ear. "You can brag all you want . . . you are a prodigy . . . Evgenia Fabianovna herself? That's amazing."

He nods slightly. "For my audition, I played a Chopin nocturne . . ." His breathing grows rough. "But, Valya, what's life without music?" He closes his eyes. He is gone.

# CHAPTER 7

The weather gets colder. The bitter weather will be as effective as our machine guns and rocket launchers against the Germans. The little Austrian corporal knows nothing about Russian winters. Last winter the Nazis suffered, and this year it will be worse for them. They don't know how to dress, and even if they did, their supplies are not coming through. The Night Witches bombed one depot full of boots and heavy clothing. The temperature drops to negative thirty degrees and the river freezes solid. My dream of crossing becomes more vivid. The airbase looms as sparkling as the Emerald City of Oz, and the frozen river is my yellow brick road.

The Germans increase their attacks, and so do the Night Witches. I look out into the frosted blackness and see the familiar formations. The trios of little planes swoop through the night to destroy the ammo dumps, supply depots, and temporary airfields that ring the city to the west.

"No Christmas for the witches. They are still riding their brooms," Yelena the butcher says as she arrives on Christmas Eve with hunks of bloody horsemeat strapped to her back.

Anna gives her a sharp look. I know she is trying to protect me. But how can I not think about my sister on Christmas Eve?

Yelena hands me a piece of horsemeat that she roasted on the camp stove. Anna announces that because it is Christmas we all will receive an extra ration of vodka.

The evening continues quietly until Gunga Din shows up with a pot of steaming soup and a wireless radio.

"You won't believe what I heard," he says breathlessly.

"What?" Anna asks.

"There's a German bunker not far from here, so we can pick up their radio broadcast from a Berlin station. I know enough German to understand. The announcer just said, 'Reporting from Stalingrad.'"

"What?" I say, and look at Anna. "There's a German newsman actually broadcasting from Stalingrad?"

"Yes, listen." He starts fiddling with the nobs and a hush falls over the trench. We all look at one another with confusion as voices begin to swell, laced with the static of the radio broadcast. It is a choir singing "Silent Night," or the German version, "Stille Nacht, Heilige Nacht."

"According to the reporter, the German army is singing this in the middle of Stalingrad. But they're lying! It's a complete deception." Gunga Din crosses his arms and glares at the radio.

"That sounds like Goebbels's work," Anna says. "Goebbels, master of propaganda."

I slide the pistol from the holster I have just put on the floor. Turning it with the muzzle pointed down, I speak into the grip as if it were a microphone. "The radio newsman and the choir are not in Stalingrad singing 'Silent Night.' We are! Russians citizens of Stalingrad. And we are not singing 'Silent Night.' We just blew up two panzers in the last hour. Not one step back!"

My comrades cheer. "Go on, Valya. Tell 'em," Anna yells.

"That voice is my commanding officer, Anna Fyodorov, and she will now sing a favorite Russian Christmas song. 'The Forest Raised a Christmas Tree.'"

> *In deep dark woods was born and raised*
> *A little Christmas tree.*
> *In winter cold and summer heat*
> *She stood all straight and green.*

By the second verse we have all joined in.

> *The snowstorm sang her lullabies.*
> *"Sleep, prettiest of trees."*
> *The forest would blanket her with snow,*
> *"Stay warm and don't you freeze!"*

We all feel better as we conclude the song.

A few minutes later we hear footsteps approaching the lounge. Rudolf, a thin boy who is a fantastic submachine gunner, enters. His face is ashen. Behind him in the immediately recognizable flat blue hat with the gold braid and a star is Comrade Commissar Sergei Malinkov of the Tenth Rifle Division. Malinkov is the second-highest-ranking NKVD officer in Stalingrad. He carries a bundle in his arms, which he drops on the ground with a thud. We gasp. It is the body of a child. A boy, perhaps eight or nine years old. There is a neat black hole in his temple. It could almost have been painted on.

"This is little Boris from the Rynok suburb. You know the fancy apartments over there?" Malinkov growls. "He became a little too friendly with the Germans' Sixteenth Panzer Division, running here and there to get them this and that, and in return they would give him a piece of chocolate." The commissar's small black eyes bore into us. "You know the child traitors, the Hiwis, often carry weapons. This one had a grenade. I was tempted to pull the pin and blow him to bits when they brought his body in. But I wanted an example. That is a Russian bullet in the boy's head." He scanned the small gathering in the lounge. "You understand. You are to shoot on sight if you see any suspicious behavior that might suggest a Hiwi."

I stare at him, horrified. "But if it's a child, how can we be sure?" As soon as the words are out of my mouth I know I have made a terrible mistake. His eyes are cold and steady and cruel. A smile crawls out from the corners of his mouth.

"And what, may I ask, is your name, comrade?"

"Comrade Valentina Petrovna Baskova."

"I will remember that." He turns on his heel to leave and then glances over his shoulder at the child's body on the floor. "I suggest that you place him on the breastworks. I noticed that they needed some strengthening." He pauses briefly. "Merry Christmas."

It is near dawn of Christmas Day. I am so agitated by the commissar's remarks that I cannot sleep so volunteer to take a double shift serving the DP-28s. My hands are red and stiff with cold. Rudi, who has taken Mikhail's place on the machine gun, leaves for his break but immediately comes back from the lounge, looking frightened.

"Comrade Valentina. There's another NKVD here to see you."

A pit of fear forms in my stomach, but I keep my voice calm. "I'm right in the middle of reloading here."

"I'll take over." I feel his eyes following me. *Off to the gulag*, I think.

I brace myself for the towering figure of Commissar Malinkov, eyes aglow with malice as he announces my arrest, but as I enter the lounge, I inhale sharply. Yuri! What in the world is he doing here? My surprise ices over into fear as I remember that, of course, snipers are part of the NKVD. Commissar Malinkov must have reported me as a collaborator, and now Yuri is here to arrest me. Or worse. If only I could have gotten across the river to Akhtuba. If only I were in the air flying over this damn city and not trapped in a trench.

Despite my growing panic, I fight to keep my composure. "Did they send you for me? I . . . I won't blame you."

Yuri blinks. "Blame me for what? What are you talking about?"

Perhaps noticing the fear in my eyes, he takes my hand and squeezes it. I stare at the dozens of rounds of sniper bullets in the straps of his bandolier. Little death birds eager to fly.

"Valya, what's wrong?"

"Your boss was here. I said something inappropriate."

He looks confused. "What?"

"Do you want me to repeat it?"

He keeps holding my hand. "No, I want you to come with me."

"Where? To the gulag?"

"No, not the gulag. You're going across the river."

"What?" I've been waiting so long to hear these words they barely sound real.

He gives me a rare grin. "Think of it as a Christmas present from Yevdokiya Bershanskaya."

"Yevdokiya Bershanskaya," I repeat, my voice full of awe.

"Yes, Yevdokiya Bershanskaya, the commander of the 588th, the Night Witches. And actually, Comrade Malinkov was most helpful."

"Malinkov? I thought he was suspicious of me."

"He *was* suspicious of you," Anna says, walking up to join us. "I didn't want him to get the wrong impression of you when he came in with that Hiwi body, so I followed him out and told him that you were the one who blew up the super panzer."

Yuri nods. "Yes, when he heard that, he agreed to let me escort you to the 588th's base."

After so much disappointment, it's hard for me to comprehend this kind of news. "How will I get across the river?" I ask, thinking about the bombs and gunfire that have been raining down on the city for months.

"Don't worry, I'll get you across," Yuri says. "Why are you looking doubtful? Aren't I the best sniper in Stalingrad?"

"Yes. Which means you probably have a big fat target on your back."

Yuri laughs. "Go get ready. It's time for you to fly."

# CHAPTER 8

When Yuri and I reach the river, I see the jackknifed hull of the ferry that was blown up almost two months ago. Staring at it, I can't keep myself from imagining the bodies still trapped inside.

I turn to Yuri. "I'm sorry."

"Sorry for what?"

"I was so angry that day."

"I understand, Valya." He smiles, and his face softens, making him look less like a sniper and more like a boy. More like someone I could care for, if he'd let me. If the war hasn't broken that part of us.

"You saved my life. And . . . and I never thanked you," I say. He takes my hand and presses it to his mouth. Is this a kiss? My stomach turns with as much confusion as excitement.

"There is no need to thank me. I should thank you."

I laugh. "Are you kidding?"

"No." His brow creases. "I don't kid about this stuff. You see, I'm a sniper. I kill all day, all night long. But I got to save you. Save a life. I felt human again." He pauses, then adds, "Briefly."

I feel tears begin to tremble in my eyes, but before I can say anything, the corners of his mouth crinkle up into a grin and he continues. "But don't thank me yet. You still might be killed flying those little toy planes. And then all my work will be in vain."

"Don't worry. I'm a pretty good pilot."

"And I'm a pretty good sniper."

He wraps his arms around me and we hold each other tightly, as if we were two drowning people hanging on for dear life.

# PART TWO

# CHAPTER 9

On the east side of the river, we climb into a jeep, and Yuri and I are driven to an airfield forty kilometers east. The land is a barren white expanse cut by the single road that we follow. Occasionally we pass a shed or small building, but the structures become fewer and fewer as we travel farther from the docks. After about half an hour, I make out a cluster of low buildings in the distance. It is an aerodrome. I feel a wonderful stirring, and I'm almost tempted to cross my fingers as I draw closer to my goal with each passing second.

The jeep stops and Yuri and I jump out. No one is there to meet us, but standing by a Yak-7 is a tall woman gesticulating fiercely as she argues with a sergeant. "Those were not my orders. I was instructed to deliver Division Commissar Boris Luvovich to the temporary airfield."

"Well, Comrade Lieutenant, there is war. Orders change. You are to deliver this young woman to the temporary airfield." The sergeant hands her some papers. She looks at them briefly and scowls.

"What young woman?"

"That one there." The man looks at a clipboard. "Comrade Valentina Petrovna Baskova."

The woman looks at me, then strides over, fury in her eyes. "Her! This little *princesa*?" Her nose wrinkles as if smelling something foul. "Her!" she says again with utter contempt.

"She's joining the ground crew. They're short on mechanics."

She scoffs, turns on her heel, and throws down the papers. "You're going to be short on something else. Take me to your commanding officer."

"As you please, Lieutenant." He leads her into a nearby shed.

Yuri and I look at each other. "Something tells me this might take a while," Yuri says, lowering himself onto a bench. After a minute or two, the man comes back out, glances at us, then merely shrugs and walks on. We can hear loud voices erupting inside. A quarter of an hour passes. Another man arrives and heads into the shed. There is more shouting. *So they need ground crew,* I think. Not pilots. Well, it's still better than being in a trench.

I try to imagine myself working with the Night Witches, and I'm so absorbed, it takes me a moment to notice that Yuri is holding the papers that the lieutenant flung on the tarmac. He raises one eyebrow as if to say, "How long do we have to listen to them argue?"

The sergeant reappears. "So?" Yuri calls. "Can we go now?"

"Not yet. They have to call Central to clear some details and fill out paperwork. The lines are down and we can't get through."

"How long will that take?" Yuri asks. "It's already getting dark."

The sergeant shrugs. "An hour, maybe two, three, maybe a day."

"A day!" I gasp.

The sergeant turns and walks back to the hut. Yuri slides the flight papers onto my knees. "This is all the paperwork you need. The Yak's been fueled."

I stare at him. "Are you serious? I can't just take the plane."

"Why not? By the time they finish the paperwork, you'll be long gone."

"But what will happen to you? You'll get in big trouble."

"A sniper get in trouble. Never!" He laughs bitterly. "I'll tell them I went to take a piss and you got away."

We walk side by side to the Yak-7. I'm so full of energy and nerves, and I can barely keep from bouncing, but Yuri is entirely calm.

"By the way," he asks, "you ever fly one of these things?"

"Of course. My father used them for teaching at Engels."

We don't say good-bye. As I walk around the plane, doing my preflight checks, Yuri seems to evaporate into thin air, just as he materialized *out* of thin air when I first noticed him in our apartment. He's a master of invisibility, and I don't blame him for it. This war has forced us to say enough good-byes to last a lifetime.

There's a flight helmet in the backseat, and goggles for the passenger who is supposed to fly in the back. Well, that passenger is not me, nor Division Commissar Boris Luvovich. And the pilot is not that screaming shrew of a lieutenant. I can still hear voices arguing, but then I turn on the engine and it purrs to life, drowning them out with my favorite sound in the world. I brake with one foot and turn, then press the rudder pedal with the other. As I begin taxiing down the runway, I look at a rearview mirror and smile. What a way to run a war. Once I have enough speed, I pull on the stick and the nose of the plane lifts into the darkening sky.

The Darlings' nursery window has indeed blown wide open, and I feel myself jumping on the back of the wind. I can't stop grinning. I'm in the pilot's seat of a Yak-7 trainer, the very plane that the all-women regiments of the 122nd trained in at Engels, where my father instructed. Bigger than the little U-2s of the Night Witches, it is heavily armed, with two UBS machine guns on the cowling. The cockpit is closed, not open, as on the U-2s. But it doesn't matter. I can still feel the wind, intuit the edges of a breeze. I have the flight plan—second star to the right and straight on till morning.

I wonder if Wendy ever looked back. Did she ever think about what she had left behind? She must have loved her mother and her father, and of course Nana, the dog.

But I have been leaving our own Number 14 in Stalingrad since the day Mama died. The first time Mama ever read *Peter Pan* to me, she pointed out the address. "Same as ours, little pumpkin." There is no one to call me little pumpkin anymore.

I shake my head and reprimand myself for such thoughts. I cannot afford to loiter within my grief, picking over my losses like a miser might pick through trash looking for lost gold. Now I must concentrate on being both pilot and navigator. The coordinates for the temporary airfield are clearly marked on the navigation chart, a secret airfield near the Northern Caucasus. It is behind the enemy lines, behind where the cauldron, the *kessel*, encloses the Sixth Army of the Nazis.

I feel a flutter in my stomach. I was of course much closer to the enemy when I was in the trenches in Stalingrad. I've seen the guns of those panzer tanks close up. I know the cold dark eye of death staring us down. Now I'm thousands of meters in the air. So which way would I prefer to die? Raked from the sky by a Stuka and explode into a burning fireball? Or blown to pieces on Gvardeyskaya Street in Trench 301? I try to shove these thoughts aside and concentrate on flying.

The moon reflects off the snow, but even this lovely sight isn't enough to mask the wreckage of war. Beneath me I can see a bombed village that is still smoldering. A forest to the south of the village appears like a graveyard of charred tree stumps.

Still, I can't keep from grinning as I gain elevation. It feels so good to fly after so long. For the first time since Mama died, I remember what it's like to feel joy.

The fizz of exhilaration turns to ice as I see the shadow of the gull-swoop wings of a Stuka printed against the rising moon. The broken cross brands the silver light. I've played out this scenario countless times in my head, but this is different. My heart thuds against my rib cage like a trapped bird, and cold dread seeps through my body. Pulling back on the stick, I plunge into a steep dive. I see the German pilot turn and my stomach plummets. He's going to chase me. He doesn't even know me and he wants to kill me.

My first instinct is to cut my speed. If only I were in a U-2 I could go so slow that the Stuka would fly too fast to aim at me. But it's too late. I'm in his crosshairs.

If I don't do something, I'm going to die.

I suddenly remember that my Yak-7 carries a pilot-operated cannon that fires through the propeller spinner. But this has to be my last resort. My best chance at survival is to outfly him. Although the Yak does not have the low-speed capability, it's as maneuverable as a hummingbird.

I pull back on the stick and head straight up, then continue in the vertical so I'm looping down again, no banking. There are stars at my knees and the charred tree stumps seem to all but scrape my flight helmet. The infamous Stuka siren begins to sear the air. But I'm used to this. This was the wailing sound we heard over Stalingrad night and day for months. It was specifically designed to unnerve the enemy. But now, with a Nazi pilot chasing me at three hundred kilometers per hour, the shrill noise rattles my bones.

My loop briefly confused him, allowing me to elude him for perhaps thirty seconds. But he's coming in again. I make a quick decision. I'm going to roll. I drop into a steep slicer turn. I'm sacrificing a lot of altitude here, but there's much to gain. I can cut the corner of the Stuka's attack line. He'll overshoot, putting me directly below him so I can come up firing.

*Don't fire too soon,* I tell myself. *Not yet . . . not* yet. I'm so close to his plane, I can almost touch it. But seconds later I hear an explosion. How is that possible? My hand's not even on the cannon trigger. The Yak wobbles as if caught in a patch of rough air. I glance down and stare, startled. On the ground I see the Stuka; its tail with the broken cross sticks up into the night. He has crashed. There's another explosion, and the smell of petrol wafts into the cockpit. Within seconds the Stuka is engulfed in flames. I hear my father's voice: "I tell those cadets to be a bomb miser. Never waste them. The Motherland does not like waste. Out*fly* the enemy."

*I outflew him. Papa!* I think. *I did it!*

The Nazi crashed. He crashed chasing me but I'm right side up in the sky now. All is in order. The moon and the stars are where they are supposed to be. Papa would be proud.

I change course and head southwest, then begin a banking turn. I can see the tanks of the Russian Sixty-Fourth Army beneath me. Another Yak flies into an escort position beside me. We are about twenty kilometers from the southern boundary of the *kessel*. I haven't felt this safe in months. We continue due west and soon are over the Fifty-Seventh Army, which is holding the southwest corner of the *kessel*. The escort leaves me. I'm on my own.

I switch off my torch, since it ruins my night vision. My only navigational aids are rivers and railroad tracks. There is a river that feeds into the Don, so I am pretty sure I'm on course.

I descend to two hundred meters. A minute later, I can make out some small huts. There are no landing lights, of course. How could there be this close to the *kessel*? At best there might be someone on the field smoking a cigarette.

I circle once, then come in for a landing, letting out a sigh of relief when the wheels thud against the ground. This is like no airfield I've ever seen. The runways are mere rutted fields. There are no hangars, and planes are huddled out near the takeoff strips. Guy wires anchor them to the ground in defense against the strong winds. The only buildings are a half dozen or so crude wooden shedlike structures. "Temporary" seems like an extravagant word to describe this airfield. Perhaps "instantaneous" is more appropriate, for it could most likely be torn down and reassembled in a matter of hours. The field is swarming with mechanics and all sorts of support vehicles, and two U-2s land behind me before I even have time to cut the engine. It seems like bedlam to me as I taxi to a halt.

As I step out of the Yak, a voice shouts to be heard over the din.

"Baskova, what are you doing out here? You're not a mechanic."

Then another voice comes. One heart-wrenchingly familiar. "I'm a *sister!*" And there she is—Tatyana, her curly bright red hair flying out from the edges of her *ushanka*. She is like my own red star in the night. I rush into her arms. I know I have to tell her about Mama first thing, but I'm already sobbing and can't get the words out.

It has begun to snow heavily. Tatyana half drags me against the wind toward a shelter. I suppose I should also tell them I "borrowed" this Yak. But I'll explain later. I'm crying too hard to speak.

"Let's get you out of the wind." She stands back and takes me in. Her eyes travel from the crown of my head to my feet. "My God, girl, you have grown! You're three inches taller than me! Whoever heard of a growth spurt in a besieged city?" She laughs. I try to laugh but can't. All I can think is that Tatyana doesn't know that Mama is dead. I'm tempted to lie, because until you know a person is dead, they are not exactly dead. You can still imagine talking to them, writing a letter. Savoring a small detail to share with them when you return. There's a terrible hole in my world, but not yet in Tatyana's.

She stares at me, and I can tell she's noticed something. My expression must have betrayed me.

"What is it, Valentina?"

I shut my eyes so I can't see her face, then lean in to whisper, "Mama was killed . . . a bullet in her throat." I feel my sister's body go rigid, racked with a sob that is about to burst. Then she goes limp in my arms.

# CHAPTER 10

The shelter is a stable. Over the doors is a sign: Flying Horse Hotel. We stay huddled outside of it for several minutes, hugging each other, sobbing.

Tatyana pulls away. "How? How did she die?" Her voice is raw, like a fresh wound.

"Sniper."

"But how?"

"She . . . she leaned out to ask Polina if the baby was all right." It sounds so innocuous.

I see it all in Tatyana's eyes. The shock that a gesture of banal kindness could have caused her death. I also see a shadow of guilt. I fold Tatyana into my arms and she presses her face against my shoulder. I'm taller. But what does it matter?

Someone calls from inside. "Come in, for God's sake. You'll freeze out there." It takes us a moment to collect ourselves, and as Tatyana steps back from my embrace, I feel hollow and empty.

As we step inside, I see a group of women bent over

embroidery hoops. It's such a strange sight, it takes a moment for it to register. "What are they doing?" I whisper to Tatyana. She looks at me as if she doesn't quite understand my question. She is sniffling and her eyes are red with tears.

"What do you mean? Doing what?"

"Them, over there."

"Oh, embroidery," she replies, as if it's the most natural thing in the world to see aviators embroidering in an old stable. "We all find it relaxing."

"What do you embroider?"

"Our underwear; scarves mostly. Really anything." She puts her hand on my shoulder, gives it a squeeze, and looks into my face. I know what she's searching for—Mama. Everyone always said that I looked so much like Mama and Tatyana like Papa. "What about Babushka?" She knows the answer even before I shake my head slowly. "Gone?" she says. I nod. "So it's just us," she whispers.

"Just us," I repeat. She takes my hand and leads me over to an oil drum that has been cut down to use as a wood-burning stove. Three women are gathered around it, warming their hands. Their goggles hang around their necks. They are obviously between missions.

"Welcome to Flying Horse Hotel." A beautiful woman of perhaps twenty-two walks over to us. She is holding a piece of fabric with little blue flowers embroidered on it. The blue flowers match the blue of her eyes. She's tiny with silvery-blond curls that remind me of a Christmas-tree angel. When my mother was a little girl before the revolution, before Tsaritsyn had been given its new name of Stalingrad, Christmas was celebrated throughout the city. Then Stalin banned all public displays, and even Christmas trees in the home were frowned upon. But Mama kept the ornaments, and on Christmas Eve we'd decorate our dinner table with figurines of Father Frost along with angels and little animals. Mara looks so much like the angel that was always perched in the center of a bronze candelabra that I'm surprised when Tatyana says, "Mara Tretorov, meet my sister Valentina. Mara is our squadron commander and holds the record for the most missions."

"That's because I've been here the longest, I think." She laughs and a blush creeps up her cheeks. "So long that I have finally finished embroidering this scarf." She holds up the embroidery hoop.

"She's very modest," my sister says. "And very musical. Mara has a beautiful singing voice. Sometimes we can coax it from her."

I nod, then glance around to look at the other women. They're all dressed in men's uniforms, though it's obvious that the trousers and jackets have all been cut down and resewed. More women straggle in. They must be the mechanics who had swarmed the field.

"Rosa was shot down tonight. Lydia saw it," one of them says grimly.

"One of our Yak-7s chased the attacker, a Stuka. Supposedly clipped it," another woman offers. She's quite tiny and has the slightly tilted eyes of a Tartar.

"Was she able to land?" someone asks.

"I'm not sure." The first woman shakes her head. "Lydia said the tail was on fire."

I try to imagine what it'd be like. The tail of your plane is on fire, near the fuel tank. You have no parachute. Rosa and her navigator seem doomed. I think of the planes I saw shot down from Trench 301. I didn't know the pilots' names. I just always hoped it wasn't Tatyana. But now I know a name other than Tatyana, and it seems horribly real.

I look around the small space. It still smells of horses. But there are no horses. There are only girls here, in their late teens to mid-twenties. Perhaps a dozen or so. The ones huddled near the oil drum have cheeks ruddy from the heat. They don't seem anxious. They appear calm but intent on whatever it is they're doing. Some sip tea. Two hold long forks with pieces of bread to toast in the fire, concentrating as if this is the most important task in the world. I have heard that in England, there's a popular slogan: KEEP CALM AND CARRY ON. That is precisely what these women are doing. This is their reality and I want to be a part of it. They are calm, efficient fighters. Then they return and quietly resume living after killing.

Tatyana leads me over to the oil drum and fetches me a mug of tea. We crouch down side by side. "I don't have long," she says. "I'm still on turnaround. Just waiting for my plane to be fueled. Then I have to go up again."

"Really?" I know the war must go on, but we've had only minutes to grieve the death of our mother.

"Yes, really."

"How many times?"

"How many missions? Eight so far tonight. I try for ten. The nights are long now. Come summer we'll be lucky to get in half that. But tonight there's no moon, so it's especially good. We call it Witch's Delight when the moon is gone. More protection. More bombs. More kills. Our mission is to destroy the arsenals that allow the Nazis to wage war. Their supplies, from weapons and bombs to food and clothing, all of it must be destroyed. Let them try to fight naked in a Russian winter, their bellies empty, their armaments demolished, their infantry decimated."

"You do that ten times a night?" She nods. "And how many of you are based here?"

"Twenty-five. That means twenty-five airplanes to be refueled and rearmed ten times each night. That's where you come in."

"Me?" I have a slightly sinking feeling. "I could be your navigator. You know how good I am with numbers." I cringe slightly. I didn't mean to sound so babyish. Like I was trying to brag about how fast I had learned the multiplication tables.

She shakes her head and gives me a tight little smile. "I

know you were quite quick when Papa was teaching us navigation."

"Very quick. Almost better than you."

"Yes." I can tell she didn't mean "Yes, I agree with you." It was just a signal to not argue with her. "Look, Valya, that was navigating on our summer holidays over the Sea of Azov. This is *war*."

I stare at her, speechless. I have spent the last four months in a city under siege. I have probably been closer to Nazis, steps away sometimes, than she has ever been in her U-2. She was flying six hundred meters above the city. I was in it!

"We desperately need ground crew," she continues.

"Really? It seemed like the field was swarming with them when we landed."

"We want to increase the number of sorties we fly each night."

"*Increase* them?" It seems impossible to me that they could fly any more than they are now. "But how can you increase them?"

"By servicing the planes more efficiently. I know I could fly more. You have to understand, loading the bombs takes at least two girls per bomb. They have to crawl on their knees with the bomb in their arms and fix it under the wing. Some nights they have to load close to three thousand kilos of bombs."

It takes all my strength to keep my voice steady. "So you're telling me that I'm not going to navigate or fly."

She nods. "We need you more on the ground than in the air. For the Motherland, Valentina."

"But, Tatyana, you know what I can do! You know I'm a great pilot."

"Valya, it's not me saying this. It's the commander. Bershanskaya."

"But I'm your sister. Can't you ask her?"

"Do you think that gives you special privileges?" She shakes her head. "Any new pilots need to be very experienced in combat. We have an astonishingly good record. Even better than the all-male units, which is why some of the officers from other regiments resent our successes. They want to introduce men into the 588th and almost enjoy hearing when one of our pilots has been shot down. So we can't risk having an inexperienced flyer. That's why we have the one thousand hours' minimum of air combat time rule."

I gasp. "That'll take years. Isn't there some other way?"

"No, Valya. It's an order, not a sisterly squabble. We need more ground crew. You're in the army now. You're a soldier. Soldiers take orders from their commanding officers. You have to grow up."

Like a harsh wind, the old arguments come back and slam me in the chest. "Another few centimeters, right?" I mutter. I can't believe we're still having the same old arguments in the midst of war. We have lost our mother and yet some things never change.

The next day, I find myself not in the air, nor exactly on the ground, but on the wing of a U-2 attempting to hold down a tarp. A blizzard with strong winds is blowing in, and all flights are canceled. Such strong winds could topple the U-2s, but with four women on each wing, we can keep the crafts grounded using special blankets, swaddling them like babies. But the wind is so strong we actually have to *lie* atop the wings to keep the planes from being blown over. One of us is a designated sweeper whose job is to sweep off any buildup of snow so we aren't smothered in a drift. However, the wind is so ferocious there is little time for any buildup.

We wrap the heaviest scarves we can find around our faces to protect us from the wind. But it's futile, as the cold from the wind, sharp as the blade of a knife, cuts through the cloth. I've heard of fingers and toes being frostbitten, turning white, then black, and then dropping off. And what about our noses? Will they be sliced off by the cold?

I'm on the starboard wing with three girls not much older than myself: Lada, Olga, and Oksana.

"Too bad we don't have Galya on our wing," Lada mutters. Galya is a very hefty girl.

"They should at least rotate her," Oksana says.

"I'll tell you who should be out here on a wing," Lada says.

"Who?" I ask.

"Nika," she giggles.

"Who's Nika?" I ask. They all laugh at this, but I don't get the joke.

"Who's Nika?" she repeats. "How long have you been here, Valya?"

"Two days."

"You prove our point," Oksana says. "Three days and she's seen not hide nor hair of Nika, our ground crew operations chief."

Lada snickers. "Nika knows more about her bottle of vodka than what's happening in the field."

Oksana sighs. "She probably wouldn't even notice if I left and became a navigator or a pilot. Not that there's the slightest chance."

"You want to fly?" I ask her.

"Of course. Who doesn't?"

"Not me," says Lada.

"Why not?" I say, surprised.

"They're all so snotty," Lada says, wrinkling her nose. "They fancy themselves so elite just because they were either heading to university or were already in one when the war broke out."

"What about you, Olga?" I ask. "Do you want to join the elite?"

"I wouldn't mind being a navigator."

"They're the worst!" Lada laughs. "You should have heard Eva going on about the opera the other day. Opera! Who has time for opera? And you, Valya? You want to be a pilot like your sister? Though I have to admit, she's not snotty."

"Yes," I answer tersely. "I want to fly."

We are strange bedfellows, or I should say wingfellows. Despite Lada's views on snotty pilots and navigators, she's a warm, funny girl. But I can tell I need to tread carefully with her.

Every half hour we are relieved and allowed to go inside to get warm and drink scalding tea. That night I manage the seemingly impossible: I scald my tongue and get frostbite on one of my thumbs. I'm ordered to suck on it, which I find funny. When I was young my mother painted a disgusting concoction on my thumb so I wouldn't suck it at night. Now here I am once more sucking on my thumb, but in the middle of a war. If I could write Yuri a letter, I would tell him not to worry. I'm not flying any planes. I'm just sucking my thumb.

# CHAPTER 11

By the following evening the weather eases and the witches are flying again. Tatyana and her navigator climb into their U-2, which I refueled. I watch as she taxis out on the so-called runway and turns the plane into the wind for takeoff. She accelerates as she bumps down the strip. I imagine her pulling back on the control stick to lift the nose. I hold my breath, tasting the envy in the back of my mouth. Her take-off is flawless. She begins to carve a turn into the night. A star gilds her wing. She is star-blessed and I'm earth-stuck. I kick the snow.

I remember flying summer holidays, when I'd climb into the rear cockpit as navigator, but also all those times when I got to be pilot and *she* navigated. I remember Papa's words: "You two are a good team, a good team!"

But now I'm stuck on the ground. I wish Papa were here. He would tell them how good I am. But Papa is gone; I'm not sure whether he's dead or alive. Mama is dead. Babushka is dead. And Tatyana is climbing high into the night.

Two more planes land for refueling. One has to fight its way through the throngs of the ground crew to get to the refueling trucks. It is the same with the bomb depots. It's quite a mess; there's very little organization. All the mechanics are in a rush.

"You learn to use your elbows," a girl named Ulla says to me as we fight for access to the pumping hoses. Our fellow mechanic Galya has certainly learned to use her elbows. She seems to take great pleasure in jabbing me in the ribs as she goes for the hoses. She would probably feel deprived if the system became more efficient. There'd be less opportunity to jab. She probably played water polo in high school.

I work all night and there is no sleep. I think a lot about Anna and the others back in the trench. They thought I was going to be flying and joked that they would wave to me as I flew over. They expected me to be up there in the sky flying, bombing, and I'm not. Did I fight my way out of the trench for nothing?

No, I know it wasn't for nothing. I'm making a contribution, no matter how small. But I can do more. My yearning to fly is stronger than ever. I crave the sharp smell of the fuel, the purr of the engines, the flutter of the prop, the darkness of the sky on moonless nights. I feel it like an ache; not in my body but in my very soul. I am meant to fly.

After a few hours of sleep, it's back to work. Even during the day when the planes aren't flying, the base is a sea of frenzied activity as we get them ready for the night raids. It is as if another war is being fought right here on the ground of our own airfield. Night, of course, is the worst, as mechanics are frantic to get their aircraft ready to turn around within minutes. When I get off duty, Ulla orders me to go to the bomb truck and find Olga and Marina, with whom I often carry bombs to the planes. I'm better at carrying than latching them to the underwing. You can't wear gloves but have to work bare-handed in order to feel what you are doing.

Just getting to the bomb truck is like diving into a pile of writhing bodies. "She's my carrier! Let her through," I hear someone yell. Then I feel a uniquely sharp jab in my ribs. Undoubtedly from the formidable elbows of Galya, whom I have learned was indeed captain of the girls' water-polo team in Leningrad. "I have to get this bomb on the squadron commander's craft. Step aside. The commander can hit five munitions depots before you move your lazy ass!" She gives another shove, and I fall backward onto the ground.

This system is ridiculous. We're going to blow each other up before we even get the bombs to the planes. If I can't fly, I can at least not get blown up or trampled by the ground crew. By the time I finally go to bed at dawn, I'm too angry to sleep. I even get paper and a pencil and make a diagram showing the paths the mechanics take between the fuel and bomb resupply stations. There are no patterns, which is half the problem. There's no cooperation. I think about the clever teamwork I saw in the sky over Stalingrad between the three

U-2s, when one plane would peel off toward the bomb site and the other two would lead a Stuka on a cat-and-mouse game through the latticework of the searchlights. That's what we need. We have to work as a team.

That evening before my shift begins I approach Mara, the squadron commander, who's sitting with the mechanic Galya and Tatyana.

I skip the preamble. "I have an idea about how to improve our system for servicing the aircraft." They look up at me.

"You've been here four days and you have an idea?" Galya mutters into her tea. Tatyana cuts her a sharp glance.

"Everyone is dead tired," I continue, pretending I didn't hear her.

"Dead tired after four days." Galya laughs.

"Shut up, Galya," Mara snaps. I'm glad it's Mara who reprimands Galya and not my sister. But I'm also surprised. Mara is so tiny and delicate, like a porcelain doll. No one would expect such a sharp tongue. But now, looking into her cornflower-blue eyes, I see a fierceness I didn't notice before. Around her neck and tucked into her flight jacket she wears the wool scarf she embroidered with little blue flowers that match her eyes. It's totally incongruous. But that, I will learn over time, is the key to Mara. It's why she's the squadron leader. She's unpredictable in the best of ways. It's why she has flown more missions than anyone, scored more hits on the best of targets.

They all look at me, obviously waiting for my idea.

"Every night, we all run back and forth between the bomb depot and the fuel truck and so on. We each have at least four different jobs that have us running willy-nilly all over the field. But what if we each were charged with one job? I know we need three armorers there to carry the bombs, since they're so heavy, but fueling requires just one person. We should have duty teams with specialized tasks who work in shifts. If Alexia did the fueling, Galya and Olga and I could focus on rearmament, and we'd have three fewer people fighting for the fuel hoses."

Galya snorts. "No offense, Valya, but let's have Alexia work on arming. You don't have the feel yet for the latching. You should do fuel."

"No offense taken." I smile. I must convince them that this will work. "You understand what I mean." They do. Even sharp-tongued Galya nods slowly.

"Let's try it tonight," Mara says.

"What's this all about?" A large, somewhat older woman comes in. It's Nika, the director of the ground crew. "What are you going to try?"

Mara steps forward. "Nika, Valya here has a proposal."

"Valya where? Who's Valya?"

Mara nods at me. "Valentina Petrovna Baskova, sister of Tatyana Baskova."

"Ah, she must be new."

"She's part of the ground crew, Comrade Nika," Tatyana explains. "And she has an excellent idea for reorganizing the ground crew operations to make them more—"

Nika cuts her off by stepping forward and jabbing her finger into Mara's chest. "You tend to the pilots, Tretorov, and I tend to the ground operations. Understand?"

Mara doesn't answer, but she scowls slightly, then turns her back and walks off a few paces.

"Understand?" Nika turns to the rest of us. No one says a word. She stomps out.

Galya swears under her breath. "Yeah, we understand, you vodka-soaked fool!" She turns to me. "It's a great idea."

"It is, Valya. Truly." Tatyana smiles.

Mara suddenly returns. "Let's do it. Nika won't know the difference."

It takes only one night to put the new system in place. On our first try, we service Mara's plane, from fueling to rearmament, in under five minutes. By the end of the evening, half the planes are being serviced by teams, greatly reducing the crowds at the fuel trucks and the bomb trucks. The airfield no longer feels like a swarming hive of bees but a rather orderly place. Despite this, there are still some hold-outs. Some mechanics and some pilots are reluctant to give up the old system.

That morning, as I'm making my way back to the Flying Horse Hotel I hear a beautiful song spooling into the frigid air. It is as if the wind has parted to make way for this thrilling voice. My heart goes still, and I stand in my too-big men's boots in snow up to my knees and listen, pulling up the earflaps on my *ushanka* despite the freezing temperatures. I don't care if my ears drop off. I recognize the song. Dvořák's "Song to the Moon" from the opera *Rusalka*. This voice is like warm honey, amber and full of light. I am enchanted. The voice begins leaping octaves, and now it burns like a flame licking away the grayness of the dawn. An overwhelming flood of joy rises within me, and when I step through the door of the Flying Horse Hotel I see Mara standing by the oil drum. In the opera, Rusalka is the daughter of a water goblin who falls in love with a prince. It's a fairy tale, and here is Mara, a Night Witch, singing it as if she were that fairy on the stage at the Mariinsky Theatre in Leningrad.

Four days later, the holdouts come to see the light, and the team system is adopted by every pilot and mechanic. In addition to creating a more orderly airfield, it allows for a shift system to be put in place, and for once we have actual designated sleeping times. A week later while I'm sleeping in the Flying Horse Hotel, someone shakes my shoulder. It's a mechanic, Alyona. I'm instantly alert.

"What is it?"

"Comrade Bershanskaya wants to speak with you."

A wave of cold dread crashed over me. "Tatyana!" I blurt out. "Has she been shot down?"

"No, no. Tatyana just landed. I saw her come in," Alyona replies.

I'm out of bed in a flash and climb into my boots. There is no such thing as nightgowns. We sleep in pants, jackets, mufflers, and hats. It's too cold for anything less.

Yevdokiya Bershanskaya is the commander of the 588th Regiment. This will be my first time meeting her. She has not been at our airfield since I arrived. And now she wants to talk to me—why? What have I done wrong?

I have to fight my way through the wind to command headquarters. It is not an imposing affair, just a hut. But it has an antenna and I notice a thermometer on the outside. The temperature is negative thirty degrees centigrade. Despite our aching bones, this makes us happy. With each drop in degree, we all almost cheer, for we know the Nazis are freezing their boots off. They have no clothes for the Russian winters and apparently have not learned from last winter. Of course our night-bomber pilots have been bombing the railway lines and supply trucks that were said to be carrying warm clothes. But the Nazi idea of warm clothes is fairly ridiculous. They simply don't know how to make them. They don't understand how the fabrics and furs must be put together in the most ingenious ways to block the cold.

There's a huge gust of wind that blasts me right through the door of the hut as I enter.

"Oh my goodness! What a wind. May it whack off the führer's privates!" Yevdokiya Bershanskaya laughs and gets up from the desk, clenching a cigarette holder in her teeth. What would my mother think if she heard how this woman so casually spoke about the führer's privates?

"Comrade Baskova, I am so pleased to meet you." She leans across the desk and extends a gloved hand.

"It is an honor, Comrade Bershanskaya."

She is a beautiful woman with warm, intelligent, laughing eyes. Another gust of wind whips through the door. "Ah, and here comes your sister." She gives a nod to Tatyana. I'm suddenly very nervous. Why is my sister here? Has Papa been found, found dead or captured? But Bershanskaya's manner is hardly that of one about to announce dreaded news. She's positively jolly.

"So, my dear, you seem to have beaten me to it." She rocks back on the heels of her boots, then quickly gestures to a chair. "Come sit down, Valentina. May I call you Valentina?" Tatyana leans against the wall. A funny half-smile plays across her face.

"Yes, or Valya," I say in a small voice. "What have I beaten you to?" She sits down again and props her boots up on the desk.

"The new servicing system. When I landed tonight it seemed that this field was more like a croquet court. No more helter-skelter. My plane was serviced in less than five minutes. I couldn't believe it." A quick smile flashes across her face. "And I am told that you are the genius behind this." I shrug. "Don't be modest. I've been trying to organize our system for ages, and you did it your first week here! You made the ground crew work as an efficient assembly line."

I feel a quiet thrill, just the way I did when Mara agreed to try my approach. Now Comrade Bershanskaya, the commander of the 588th, is praising me. I only wish Nika was in the small room to hear her.

The commander pauses a moment. "I like to think that I also introduced an assembly line of sorts, one for training pilots and navigators, so we can continuously feed the regiment and keep us operational and all female." I feel a flicker of excitement but say nothing. "I want to begin training mechanics and armorers to become navigators." Her voice quickens as she speaks. "And then train navigators to become pilots."

The flicker grows into a blaze. This could be my chance. "I'm now on refueling, but I can already fly."

"I know that, my dear, but have you ever flown in combat?"

"No."

"Well, let me tell you that the best way to learn is to navigate. And I know you know how to do that as well." She casts a glance toward Tatyana. "Your sister tells me that you scored higher than she did on the navigation test in the aero club."

"She did?" I look around and see Tatyana still leaning against the wall. Her face is inscrutable, yet still there is the odd smile.

"Always feels good, admit it," Bershanskaya chuckles, "to beat an older sister."

"Well, navigating isn't quite the same as being a pilot," Tatyana interjects.

I ignore her patronizing remark. "When will I begin?"

"Tonight. Is that soon enough?" She smiles. "You'll fly with the squadron commander, Comrade Mara Tretorov."

I'm so overwhelmed, I can barely speak. "Yes, comrade . . . and . . . and thank you for this opportunity."

"I should thank you. You are helping to get our fragile little U-2s up there faster than we ever thought possible. We have increased our sorties by one third in these last few days. Be proud. Be proud you are a soldier. Be proud you are a woman." She tips back in her chair and points at the banner that hangs on the wall. In flowing writing it reads "You are a woman, and you should be proud of that." That is the slogan of the 588th Regiment. And I realize I'm proud to be a woman and proud to be a navigator. My first step toward being a pilot!

# CHAPTER 12

*I'm getting closer.* That's all I can think when I climb into the rear cockpit a few hours later, for the first of eleven sorties with Mara. Our first target is a railroad line leading toward Stalingrad. There's a Nazi depot near the railroad supposedly filled with warm clothes, food, and munitions. We are flying in the first bomber position. This means we will drop the first bomb on the target while two other planes fly decoy to distract the German antiaircraft fire. Destroying depots like these is key. If they don't have the food or warm clothes, they will have to retreat. This is just the kind of target Night Witches love.

"If we drop these bombs right, the munitions stored in that depot will do the rest of the work. The place will go up like a barn full of dry hay," Mara shouts back to me.

We are flying in a line with two other planes. How often I have watched this formation from the ground in Stalingrad. My eyes are fastened on the compass and the coordinates on the map. I kill my torch one kilometer from the target. I feel Mara throttle back. The sky is suddenly latticed with light. It feels as if we have entered an electric spiderweb.

"Altimeter twelve hundred meters," I call.

She begins her descent and we slow to a glide speed. To drop the bomb we must not be below six hundred meters. Any lower and the blowback from the explosion will damage our own aircraft. We begin crawling into one of the few dark spaces between the searchlights. Meanwhile, the other two U-2s are being harassed by tracer bullets. I think my heart is beating louder than our notoriously quiet engines, which at this speed are almost mute. One U-2 peels off and bombs a searchlight. We feel the reverberations but keep flying through our dark channel. A tremendous thrill floods through me as Mara throttles back and the engines quiet to a near idle and we soundlessly close in on the target. We are deadly, yet I have never felt more alive. Is this how Yuri must feel when he draws the helmeted head of a Nazi into the crosshairs of his rifle? Fifty seconds from the target. I look at the painted mark on the wing. This is the system for lining up the target. When the mark and the target overlap, I pull the handle of the bomb release. There is a slight jolt, then a huge blast. The little plane shakes so violently, I could swear we were below the minimum six hundred meters. The conflagration roils up into the night like a breaking sea of flames. Mara accelerates and we climb into the storm of antiaircraft fire, where the air is thick with the scent of explosives.

We head to our second target, both decoy planes with us once again. We're meant to hit a fuel depot right on the edge of the front. The searchlights frighten me more than anything. It's like flying through a deadly maze. But our next target, a German staff headquarters near Mozdok, has even more powerful searchlights. After I pull the bomb latch we are caught in the beam for a few seconds and it's blinding. I see Mara slouch down in the cockpit, for she can see nothing outside for several seconds even after we escape the beam. It's hard maintaining a level flight and we seem to waggle about. We drop our last bomb. Mara climbs back up and begins to initiate a steep turn toward our base.

Our strategy tonight is what we call a tight shuttle. With three craft we weave in and out as we drop our loads of bombs. Rotating the first bomber position among the three of us, we are joined in a dark dance of death. It is like a rondo, except the music is gunfire coupled with the sizzling rasp of tracer bullets and the percussion of the bombs. Destroying a searchlight gives me as much pleasure as blowing up munitions depots and bridges.

There are linked controls between the two cockpits, and by our third sortie Mara is tired, and turns the flying over to me for the return trip. She begins singing an old Russian folk song, "Katyusha," the song for which the rocket launcher was named.

*Apples and pears had blossomed,*
*The river was cloaked in fog.*
*A shore that was steep and forbidding*
*Katyusha came out atop.*

*She sang of a bluish-gray eagle*
*That flew in the vast, silent steppe;*
*She sang of the one she held dear,*
*Whose letters she carefully kept.*

*Oh song, little song of a maiden,*
*Go follow the sun in the sky.*
*A fighter you'll find in the trenches—*
*Please tell him Katyusha says hi.*

*A sight of this girl, of her singing*
*You shall in his mind resurrect.*
*And while he's protecting the country,*
*The love will Katyusha protect.*

It is soothing. Her voice twines through the thrum of the engine. Like a flower-laden vine, it climbs through the night, blooming in the darkness. But as I fly the tiny U-2, leaving the flames of Stalingrad behind, I cannot help but wonder about my friends in Trench 301. I think of Mikhail, my little commander. Why had he never mentioned he was a pianist?

Is Anna still head of the trench? Does Gunga Din bring water; and the butcher girl, where is she with her slabs of horsemeat? Yuri, Yuri, my dear sniper; who is in his sights this evening? I feel a funny little stir in my heart when I think of him. A tenderness for a killer. We are all killers in one sense, whether we drop bombs from the sky or fire anti-aircraft guns from a trench, but Yuri is the only one who sees the face of the intended victim when he draws him into his sights. I never saw the faces of the German soldiers who died when I dropped the bombs on the searchlights. All I thought about was the thrill of seeing the light blink out and the calm swell of darkness swim up into the night. I didn't give a thought to their burned bodies, their last gasps of air. I only experienced joy at having taken out one filament in the electric spiderweb of the horribly illuminated light of war.

I am haunted by those bittersweet words of the song: "Let him remember an ordinary girl." Would Yuri remember me? I remember him so well. The perfect innocence in those keen eyes. His words come back all of a sudden, and I break out in a cold sweat. *You see, I'm a sniper. I kill all day, all night long. But I got to save you. Save a life. I felt human again.*

But now I have killed. I have probably killed more people in this single night with our 250 kilos of bombs than he could kill in a week with his little rifle. Every time I pulled that handle to release the bomb, I delivered death wholesale. Am I still human?

# CHAPTER 13

The war does not end on February 2, but the Battle of Stalingrad does. I am grateful. It means the killing has stopped. Of course I don't know which of my friends, my teachers, or my neighbors survived these months of hell. But now we have the Germans on the run—running west—and we, the Night Witches, will follow them "like flies on rotting meat," as Bershanskaya says.

The Battle of Stalingrad is over, but not the war. We like to think of the Nazis in retreat, fleeing with their tails between their legs. However, they are more like mad dogs with their teeth bared, more perilous than they have ever been. They rape, they burn. Their rage is fed by the humiliation of their defeat at Stalingrad.

Before we turn west, Mara is ordered to fly over the crippled city and report back to Bershanskaya on the conditions.

The morning is thick with fog that melts away as a bright sun rises. Wind-whipped clouds break across a blue sky. It's the first time I've flown with her in the daytime, and there's an eerie quietness to the world. No Messerschmitts streaking across the blue of the morning. The Stukas that traveled the sky like closely packed schooling sharks have all vanished.

"Look down there, port wing," Mara shouts. It's the Pitomnik airbase that the Nazis took four months ago. Now it is in shambles. The carcasses of two dozen Stukas and countless Messerschmitts, along with the gargantuan Focke-Wulf Condors, lie shattered on the ground. How I trembled just two weeks ago when one of those condors screamed out of the night. Mara had called back, "Don't worry." Then she immediately cut her speed and the Focke-Wulf overshot us instantly, leaving Mara and me far behind in its wake. We told that story with glee when we returned.

"Like David and Goliath!" Olga hooted.

"No, more like the tortoise and the hare," I said. Then Leah, who specializes in repairing the ailerons, the flaps, and the movable parts of the wings, took it upon herself to paint a tiny tortoise near the red star on the fuselage of our plane.

I noticed that everyone seemed buoyant about our tale of losing the Focke-Wulf, except for Tatyana, who looked very serious. "It takes a lot of skill to throttle back under those circumstances because of the turbulence caused by a Focke." She spoke to Mara, but I knew the remarks were addressed to me. Translation: Little sister, you are nowhere near that level of skill yet.

On this bright morning as we approach Stalingrad, we see signal flares shooting into the sky from the city's center to herald the surrender of the German Sixth Army. Sailors from the Volga flotilla make their way across the frozen river with bags of bread and food for the survivors, who have been trapped for months. We dive low, flying over streams of people moving slowly through the ruined city. A few wave at us. But even from this distance I can see they are stunned. Stunned that it's finally over. But there is no cause for jubilation. Stalingrad seems more like a living corpse than anything else.

"Wait!" I say. "Bear two points east, then south."

"What is it?"

"The statue."

"What statue?"

"The children dancing around the crocodile. It still stands!"

"All six children?"

"Every single last one of them," I say quietly, thinking of all the real children they outlasted. I remember climbing on that statue with Tatyana. It was a wonderful stage for our make-believe games, perfect for Peter Pan since the crocodile that ate Captain Hook's hand was the centerpiece of the sculpture. We'd pretend to be Peter and Wendy and "fly" over the crocodile's head by leaping about. But then one day the make-believe stopped. I remember that day so clearly. It was bitterly cold, but cold had never distracted us before.

"I don't want to play anymore," Tatyana had said abruptly.

"Why?"

"Because."

"Because why?"

"Because it's stupid."

"It's not stupid," I had protested.

"Make-believe *is* stupid. I'm too old."

I had stood there in disbelief, staring at my sister. She seemed rooted to the pavement, and as I looked at her, I could almost see our childhood receding in front of my very eyes, pulled out by an immense tide. And I wasn't quite ready for whatever came next.

Later we are told that nearly two million people died in the Battle of Stalingrad, and many of them were children. By the end of the battle there were just 997 children left in the city, and only nine of those would be reunited with their families. But these six little figures dance around the crocodile in shameless eternity. What's wrong with God? Was this some kind of joke?

We circle the monument once, then head back to the base.

The night after the German retreat is Mara's and my first night off since I began flying with her. Our airbase is nearly empty, as another base is being set up farther to the south and west. We are not sure where at this point, as the exact location is never confirmed until just before the move. Mara shakes her head wearily.

"What is it?" I ask, but I think I know. We both feel a profound exhaustion from seeing the wreckage of what had been a beautiful city.

"Do you think we will ever remember what it was like

before the war?" she whispers into the fire, where she is toasting a piece of bread on a stick.

"I remember, but I don't quite believe what I remember."

"Tell me what you remember." So I tell her of our family's holidays on the Sea of Azov, of Christmas and the Christmas angel that looked just like her.

She laughs softly. "I'm no angel."

"I never said you were. I said you looked like one. There's a difference."

"Don't I know it." She says it so emphatically that my interest is piqued. I raise an eyebrow, and she quickly says, "Oh, I wasn't exactly a devil. But let's just say a naughty angel."

"What does a naughty angel do?"

"Fool around with a lot of boys."

"Really?"

"Yes, really."

"You know what's sad?" I say.

"What?" She looks at me with those lovely cornflower-blue eyes.

"I haven't had time to be a naughty angel."

She smiles sweetly. "You're still so young. I'm twenty-two. There's time."

"Yeah," I say. "But there's a war."

She doesn't argue, but the wistful look in her eyes says it all.

# CHAPTER 14

From the air, it looks like the teeth of a shark are ripping up from the earth and devouring the land. It's the German fortified line, Blue Line, bordering the straits that separate the Black Sea from the Sea of Azov. It's studded with antiaircraft batteries, machine guns, and the dreaded searchlights. But now, for the first time, some of our own U-2s have machine guns mounted behind the navigator's cockpit, facing the rear for firing. We are no longer just dropping bombs. If a Nazi fighter plane tries to give chase, we can fight back more aggressively.

I spend a week learning how to fire the gun on the ground at our temporary airfield on the Taman Peninsula. In the plane, the gun is mounted on a swivel on the back of the navigator's cockpit. My experience as a loader in Trench 301 doesn't help me with this new gun. The vibrations from the U-2's engine make the crosshairs dance around, and I can't tell you how many bullets I fire drop into the Black Sea. I never make my mark. Then, on the sixth day practicing in the air, I finally make my first hit. A minute later, I see a piece shoot off from our fuselage. Little do I know it was less than a meter from the petrol tank. We could have gone up in flames and dropped right into the Black Sea. But at the time, Mara and I had no idea it came so close to the petrol. If we had, I doubt I could have had the wits to fire the machine gun so straight.

This happens about ten days after our regiment, the 588th, is redesignated as the Guard Night Bomber Regiment. Our goal is to recapture Malaya Zemlya, or Little Land, as it is called, near Novorossiysk. This is considered a key target. If we wipe out the Germans at Little Land, a gate will swing open to the west and the Germans will scamper like rats deserting a sinking ship.

We're near a fishing hamlet not far from where my family took our summer holidays before the war. The airfield is on a narrow strip of beach, near a cluster of small structures that in the summer are used as bathing huts. Our naval infantry is holding strong against fierce German attacks, and our mission this night is to drop food and medical supplies for our troops near the Blue Line, or the shark's mouth, as I think of it. I'm excited for this mission. It's the first time we have not been charged to destroy something. But I'm still not piloting. I yearn to be the one pushing on the control stick, lowering the nose for a dive. The longing is so intense, it's like an ache in my muscles. It seems wrong that I'm not a pilot. I overhear Bershanskaya saying how desperate the 588th is for pilots, but they demand that we accumulate those devilish one thousand hours of combat flight time as navigators before we can advance! It's ridiculous, especially since we fly only at night. As spring approaches, the nights become shorter and the days longer, which makes it impossible to accumulate the required hours. I won't be able to really begin stacking the hours until autumn comes, which drives me insane.

As we approach our destination, we see the bonfires of the men in our naval infantry—the ones waiting for us to drop supplies. But before we get low enough to perform the drop, one of the dreaded Nazi searchlights floods the sky with harsh light. They've spotted us, and now they're opening fire from the ground. Mara throttles back and calmly goes into a glide toward the beach. I pull on the bomb release handle, but of course there are no bombs, only crates of tinned food and medicine. I lean over and wave at the sailors, who wave back. They shout, "Thank you, dear witches! Thank you!"

And then one calls out, "Not witches! You are our heavenly angels." And I bless the odd little engine, which is so quiet that we can hear their shouts from the ground.

I feel a surge of joy like I've never experienced throughout the war. I imagine the soldiers opening the tins of sardines, biscuits, and chocolate, licking their fingers as they enjoy this feast we have delivered.

We make several passes. I love releasing the packages. It is delicious, as if I'm tasting the chocolate with them. It's almost like we've gathered at some magical table halfway between sky and earth and are having a party together. The table is beautiful, set with starlight instead of candles.

I'm just releasing the last container when there is a terrible lurch that sends my stomach plummeting. My reveries are finished. Everything is sliding off the table. I hear the awful thud of bullets against the fuselage. Mara has lost control of the plane. We are dipping and heading straight for the ground.

The land is askew. I am askew. My feet are in the air. And the air is thick with black smoke. I can hardly breathe. Everything begins to shudder. No one is piloting the plane.

*Chert voz'mi!* I curse, and then see that Mara is slumped over the steering column. She's been shot. My mind goes blank, and then it's as if someone else's brain takes over. A stranger, and yet this stranger has a familiar voice—mine. *I must take control of the plane. I must reach the control stick. If I fly the plane we live.*

She's blocking the control stick. I have to lean over and push her aside so I can hit the switch to transfer the control to the rear cockpit. Damn, she's blocking the switch. It's easier to grab the control stick. My hands can barely reach around her but I get a tenuous hold on the stick and pull back, taking us out of the plunge. The air is rough, and it's hard controlling the roll of the craft. Banking is nearly impossible. The ailerons must have been damaged. But at least we're right side up now. That's an improvement. Still, I have no idea how to land this beast. But the airfield isn't far. If I can just even the plane out, we might make it, but the vibrations in the control stick are crazy.

"Never mind crazy," I whisper. "I have to concentrate. Mara, I must concentrate, right?" I don't look at her. But I keep talking to her. I'm not sure what I say, but I feel if I talk to her she can't die. She must know that I am flying this craft. That I am concentrating. I can do this. But I cannot quite reach the control switch so I can fly from the rear cockpit seat. Nevertheless, in this awkward position I am managing to fly the plane. The prop is still spinning; the wings are becoming level. Yes, the plane could fall apart any second, but by God I'm going to fly it until it does. I keep talking.

"You'll be fine," I tell Mara, trying to keep the panic out of my voice. "We're almost back. Everything's going to be okay." But there is blood over everything, and deep inside of me, I know this cannot all be fine.

We are just above the airfield. Our streaming black plumes of smoke have brought people rushing out onto the field with hoses from the water trucks. The plane is now jittering insanely as I throttle back and glide, trying to line up the landing flags. Now for the final stall. I pull back slightly on the stick to lift the nose. It's unbelievable. I set this wounded bird down softly as a swaddled baby. We land. Barely a thud.

I reach over the forward cockpit seat and press my face against Mara's flight helmet. "We're here, Mara. We're here." There are puddles of blood in the seat, in her lap, everywhere.

"She's not dead," I shout as the ground crew rushes toward us. "She's not! You have to help her!" More people swarm around the plane. They extricate Mara first, and then me. The world around me spins, and for a few moments, all I can see is blood. Blood on the hatch door of the cockpit. Blood on the wing. Everything goes dark and hazy, and when I come to again, I'm being carried from the plane on a stretcher. Tatyana is jogging alongside.

"You're not hurt," she says, her face pale. "You're going to be fine."

"But the blood. So much blood."

"It's Mara's."

"She's hurt, but she'll be all right. I know it." Tatyana says nothing but keeps jogging along. The shock and numbness that had encased my body drain away, replaced by panic. I start to climb off the stretcher.

"Stay where you are," Tatyana orders.

"I'm fine. I want to see Mara," I say, staggering forward.

"No." Tatyana reaches for me, but I duck away.

The girls who are carrying the stretcher glance at Tatyana. "What are you not telling me?" I grab Tatyana's shoulders and I shake her hard.

"Mara's dead."

"Dead?" The word doesn't register as more than a sound, as if my sister has just spoken in another language. "I . . . I don't understand . . . No . . . she couldn't have died." My mind races. She was just a naughty angel. Not a devil. She can't be dead.

Tatyana gently takes my arm and guides me into the hut. The girls clear away from the fire in the oil drum. My sister fetches me a tin cup with maybe two centimeters of vodka. I take a swallow. It burns all the way down to my chest. I look at her and peer into her soft gray-green eyes. No words are spoken. But I know she senses the depth of my loss. She understands. Mara was my sky sister. My sister of the long nights. I look down. My flight vest is splattered with her blood. I wrap my arms around myself and close my eyes.

"How? How did she die?"

"Tracer bullets."

"But I wasn't hit at all."

"Yes, she took it full on." She hesitates, and I can tell she's not telling me something. I lean toward her and bring my face close to hers. My voice is hoarse. "What are you not telling me, Tatyana?"

Her hand settles at the base of her neck. "Her throat, like Mama."

And as with Mama, I picture the words of a song shattering, but this time, it is I who grabs my own throat, as if trying to catch the notes.

Tatyana puts me to bed. She must have given me a sleeping draft, for I slide into a thick, dreamless sleep.

# CHAPTER 15

I feel a brief moment of disorientation when I wake up. For the first few seconds, everything seems fine, and then reality crashes in. Mara is dead. The torn throat, the blood, the gelid blue eyes as they placed her on the stretcher. It all comes back. I must have slept for a long time—through the morning into the day, for it is night again already.

I get up from my cot, pull on my pants and boots, then walk toward the washbasin we all share. The coals in the small warming stove have gone dead, and there's a thin layer of ice on the pitcher of water. I'm the only one in the hut. Everyone is out flying, the situation more urgent than ever. Now that we've past the March equinox, we can feel the minutes being peeled from the long winter nights. That means there's less time to fly, fewer bombs to drop, fewer Nazis to kill in the dwindling darkness. And fewer hours for me to collect to become a pilot.

We are determined to obliterate the Blue Line, the shark's mouth that devoured my dear Mara. Destroy that Blue Line and the Nazis will again be on the run, as they have been since their defeat at Stalingrad. But the shorter nights leave us more exposed. We are Night Witches. We thrive in the darkness.

I walk over to Mara's empty cot and pick up her scarf. It is stained with her blood. I press it to my face. If there is any scent of Mara left, I want to inhale it. But there's nothing. Nothing except the blood. I go to the washbasin and pour cold water from the pitcher on it. Cold water is best for removing bloodstains. I remember Mama telling me this. I bend my head over the blood-swirled water in the basin and rock back and forth, murmuring her name over and over like some old Orthodox priest in combat boots. Praying? Not exactly. Prayers went away years ago, evaporated like the morning dew under the bright sunshine of communism. Who knows how to pray anymore? Within minutes the blood is gone. I'll hang the scarf out to dry and keep it, wear it myself.

I am glad that no one is around right now. I want to be alone, alone in the hollowness of the night. I put on my flight jacket and *ushanka*. Before I leave the hut I take Mara's scarf. It is still slightly damp but I tuck it in just as she did and walk out toward the airfield. In the distance the sky is jagged with flak and tracer bullets. But here at our base there's an eerie quiet. I see someone come out of the mechanic's hut and scan the night for an incoming U-2. A peculiar whine rises on the edge of the wind, the hum of a still prop. There's only one plane standing on the field, and I realize it's ours. Mara's and mine. The little craft is singing a dirge to its lost pilot.

They've already dug her grave. There were most likely some quickly muttered prayers. That's what passes for a funeral service. I've attended a few in the three months since I've been in the regiment. They use special shovels to dig into the frozen earth. I'm glad I missed Mara's burial. I don't want to think of her under all that dirt. I only want to think of her in the sky.

I look over at our plane. In that moment it seems almost animate, the hum of the propeller like the cry of an abandoned puppy. I walk over to it and touch the fabric of the upper wing lightly. How does one cuddle a small, fragile bomber?

I feel tears freezing on my face. Someone is tapping me on the shoulder. It's Tatyana.

"Commander Bershanskaya just arrived. She wants to see you." She puts her arm around my shoulders as we walk to the command hut.

Bershanskaya is studying a map, a cigarette holder clamped in her teeth. She looks up and stubs out the cigarette, sighing deeply.

"I just heard the news about Comrade Mara Tretorov. I am so very sorry." She comes out from around the desk. Her hand drops on my shoulder and she squeezes it. But her eyes are hard. "They tell me that the damage to the plane was light. It'll be repaired within a few hours. Tonight you'll fly again."

"But who will be the pilot?"

"You."

I'm too stunned to speak, but I see Tatyana's face tighten. She tucks in her lips until they are a bloodless white seam. Then she finally speaks.

"Commander Bershanskaya, my sister doesn't have the hours yet. She needs one thousand hours to—"

Commander Bershanskaya cuts her off. "I know what is required, Comrade Baskova. You don't need to inform me. I made the rules. I can break them. Be ready in an hour, Valentina Baskova."

"Yes, Commander." I nod vigorously as joy swells in me. I have an urge to jump up and down like a child. The words dancing within me threaten to burble up. *I'm going to fly. I'm going to fly.* I dare not look at Tatyana, though I feel her stare drilling into me. Will she tear off my wings? I can't let her spoil this moment for me.

"But—" Tatyana starts to protest.

Bershanskaya interrupts her again. "Your sister handled the plane beautifully when she had to take the controls from Mara. You realize that both ailerons were completely stripped. It's incredible, Valya, that you landed that plane without crashing. The craft is going to be back in the air by this evening, and *you* will be in the cockpit."

The commander draws her face closer. There is the smell

of tobacco on her breath. "Don't look so surprised. We need pilots like you. In another few days we will have destroyed the Blue Line. That's been our goal. We are closer than you can imagine. We want to see the backsides of those Nazis running, stampeding, and they will be. I promise."

I glance over at Tatyana while the commander is speaking to me. My sister's eyes are smoldering.

"Who will be my navigator?"

"Galya."

"Galya," I repeat, trying to keep the dismay out of my voice. But the commander is already walking out the door of the hut. Tatyana and I are left facing each other.

"Pleased?" she asks.

"Why did you say I didn't have the hours?"

"You *don't* have the hours. The rules were there to keep unqualified people from hurting themselves. Or others." The words like spikes of rancor make me gasp.

I glare at my sister. I am burning, burning at a low temperature. Cold fire, they call it. My chemistry teacher demonstrated the phenomenon once. It's rather like the flame in a cigarette lighter. It's basically noncombustible, but you can feel the heat. I feel the heat. But I won't blow up. Instead I turn my back and spit on the ground. That gesture is worse than any words. Sharper than any slap. And as vile as any obscene gesture. But it is cold. Cold fire.

\*   \*   \*

Galya's face is unreadable as she walks out with me to the plane later that night. My heart is beating so fiercely I'm sure she'll hear it. I can't believe that after all these months my dream is about to be realized. I'll be in the front seat at last. My hand will be on the control stick.

As we walk, the ghost of the rudder pedals brushes the soles of my feet, as if I'm about to initiate a turn. I love that feeling of slipping beautifully into a turn, finding that curve in the geometry of air and speed. One becomes a sculptor, carving the air like a bird, an eagle, an owl, a gull.

I climb into the cockpit, start the engine, and taxi down the runway. The land falls away so gradually it seems as if the plane is straining. Once we're up, I breathe a bit easier. I know that the rudder for the U-2 is huge and the response is quick. I'm worried that perhaps with the weight of Galya it might not react as quickly, so I try initiating some turns by briefly touching the rudder pedals with my feet and then banking with the control stick. It seems fine. I hear a deep raucous laugh and feel a thwack on my shoulder. "You're worried about Fatty back here!" I feel my face flush. "Not to worry. You have the right touch. You're a good pilot."

And Galya is a good navigator, even better than I was. She reads the wind indicators excellently and does lightning-fast calculations in her head. She is particularly skilled at calculating our burn rate for fuel. If we are low, she knows just how high to climb, as the engine burns less when the air is thinner. Less resistance.

I feel that I should be happier, more excited to be flying. But how can I be happy knowing that I sit where Mara sat just a day ago? There's so much at stake here. We have to finish off the Blue Line, destroy it completely. This was the German gateway into Russia two years ago. The Kerch Strait separating the Sea of Azov and the Black Sea is a scant eight kilometers across. Clasping the strait are two claws like a lobster. The eastern claw is the Taman Peninsula, and that is where the Blue Line of the German army is. That line, the shark's mouth, is spiked with antiaircraft batteries, machine guns, and searchlights—a hundred, maybe a thousand searchlights. The Blue Line runs close to sixty-five kilometers, from Novorossiysk to Temryuk.

I feel the first bite of the searchlights. Then the shark's mouth begins to spit fire. It has become a dragon!

I hear Galya cursing through the headphones. Tracer bullets from antiaircraft guns on the ground dance around me. It is a curtain of fire. I can feel the heat. Amazingly, Galya keeps calling the bearings. "Five degrees port . . . Nose up . . . Bank." Then the curtain parts and there is the white looming eye of a single searchlight. Galya reads my mind. She knows how I hate them.

"Let's launch ourselves into their sights!" she yells. We swoop down. I hear the crank of the bomb-release gears. "Geronimo!" Galya roars. There's an explosion, then an electrical crackling and sudden darkness. The sky is no longer striped with light. I carve a turn, and beneath my port wing

I glimpse a huge fire surrounding the sizzling skeleton of the searchlight.

I have no idea what *Geronimo* means. But we've destroyed the biggest of the searchlights. I'm practically euphoric. I hate those searchlights almost as much as I hate the Nazis.

When we get back, our wings are blackened with smoke. We reek of smoke. Our faces are smudged with smoke and ash except where our goggles blocked it. We look at each other and laugh. We are like reverse raccoons. Instead of dark rings around our eyes we have white ones.

"Galya, what does *Geronimo* mean? Why did you shout that when we hit the searchlight?"

"Ha! I'm becoming a Yank. It's what the American paratroopers say when they jump out of a plane."

"Why would they say that?"

"Who knows? They're Americans!"

I am so elated that for a moment I forget about my fight with Tatyana. I scan the airfield for her, desperate to tell her about my success. But then I remember, and my exhilaration turns to dust.

Tatyana and I avoid each other for several days. When we finally begin to speak, it's just terse exchanges, always in the company of others and usually pertaining to weather, or perhaps a common mechanical issue that we all experience. Nothing personal. I remember our mother saying once that people who have nothing to say to each other talk about weather. Well, that's us. It seems like a void in my life. We are both pilots now. We are both equal. Yet it feels as if a counterweight is missing.

Unexpectedly, Galya and I become close. Unlike Mara, Galya doesn't sing on our return flights, but she talks. Talks quite a bit. She has had many boyfriends. She is twenty-one and claims she was, at fifteen, the oldest virgin in her school in Rostov.

"Had to get rid of it," she says with a grin. I nod and make some sort of sound that suggests I agree with her. As if I too had to get rid of it. I can't help but think of my "naughty angel" talk with Mara just weeks before she died.

"So anybody you had to kiss good-bye?" Galya asks.

"Not exactly," I say. I try to imagine waking up in the arms of someone. No, not someone—Yuri Yurovich Vaznov.

"There was a boy that I met in Stalingrad just before I left."

"Who?"

"A sniper."

"A Stalingrad sniper?"

"Yes."

"Not Yuri Vaznov?"

I'm grateful that Galya can't see me blush from the rear cockpit. "Yes . . . him."

"Really? He's so famous! How did you meet him?"

I bite my lip. Meeting Yuri is so entwined with my mother's death, I almost feel guilty admitting I was drawn to him.

Not that I felt it right away, but it's difficult for me to sort out all the feelings surrounding how we met.

"It's hard to explain. He was hiding out in my apartment building for a couple of days."

"So?" There's almost a leer in her voice.

"So he seemed nice, and yes, I sort of liked him. That's all." I switch the intercom off and start a banking turn back to the airfield. There are some violent updrafts coming off the mountains, and along with the wind shear, they make the plane hard to control. I have to concentrate.

As we drive the enemy west, in late spring we find ourselves in a new airfield in the Kuban region in the Northern Caucasus. Rumors abound that the Allies, the British and the Americans, are planning an invasion. So now our goal is to force the Nazis right into the deadly embrace of the Allied forces waiting to greet them in the west.

The front line is just forty-five or at most fifty kilometers away from us. The mechanics and the armorers work all night refueling our craft and attaching bombs. We are squeezing in the maximum number of missions in the smallest frame of time. With the nights growing shorter and the days longer, there's not a second to waste. It's bitterly cold and there are no shelters to speak of. Only dugouts and trenches. Pilots, navigators, mechanics, armorers are all squashed together. In our furry trousers we must look like a pack of forest animals in a den. There is a smallish oil drum, a *burzhuika*, that serves as our fireplace. Our first task in this new area is to knock out the scores of searchlights that comb the sky. Then we move again.

Spring fog becomes a menace. Often we can't make it back to base and have to land in a field that we hope is not in enemy territory. We have been lucky so far. On those nights we sleep in the cockpits. I tease Galya that her snores are louder than our sewing machine of an engine. On one particular night as we sleep I hear a gentle tapping on our fuselage. I jerk awake. An elfin face with dark eyes peers into mine.

"Madame, would you like some tea?"

I inhale sharply as a younger face slides across my mind's eye. A face from what now seems a century ago. Yuri! It's as if my dear sniper friend has suddenly become an old man. But it's not him, of course. This man does not carry a rifle. He's holding a flask.

"May I?" he asks as he sets the flask on the lower wing. He then unhitches two metal cups from his belt, sets them on the wing, and begins pouring.

"Sugar?"

"Yes," Galya, who is awake now, answers for both of us. He pours about a teaspoon from a small paper cone.

"Now, I can bring you some hard-cooked eggs from my house if you like? Or perhaps you can come in?"

"We have to leave as soon as the fog clears," Galya says.

"I thought so," he replies. "The others always say that."

"Others?" we both blurt out with sudden alarm.

"Oh, don't worry. I don't serve tea to Nazi scum. They've never seen me. But several from the other women's regiments, the 586th, 125th, and now you, the first of the 588th—but I understand they call you the Forty-Sixth, the Taman Guards. The ones the Nazis call the Night Witches, but I . . . I call you Night Angels."

"Really?" I say.

"Yes, my son, who was at Azov, wrote about your food and medicine drops. The least I can do is bring you a cup of tea and a hard-cooked egg." He looks about. "Hup! The fog is lifting. Let me run off for your eggs. Be back in a tick."

I watch him totter off into the swirling scarves of mist. If he had not had that clearly Asiatic face and been dressed in farmer's overalls, I would have sworn he was a butler who had wandered in from one of the English movies Mama and Tatyana and I sometimes saw at the Illuzion Theater in Stalingrad.

By the time we have our eggs peeled, the fog has cleared off completely. I immediately start up the engine, and we taxi down what had once been a sugar-beet field. But is it worth replanting a field in the midst of war? The seeds of war seem to be the only crop that is growing. The *kessel* is working. Stalingrad has not succumbed to the Nazi Sixth Army. But outside the *kessel*, particularly in the Northern Caucasus, there are eruptions.

June is a very tough period. Searchlights comb every one of our targets. We stick to what we call our two-plane strategy, slightly different from the three-plane strategy that was used over Stalingrad. Cooperating over a target, one of us flies decoy; the other slides in at a very low altitude and speed, then blasts the hell out of the target. Most of our targets are depots—fuel ones are especially tricky, for when they explode, it is like instant inferno in the sky. Deadly walls of fire and then thick smoke. There are moments when it is impossible to tell the sky from the ground. And always there are the searchlight beams. I have become an expert at weaving through the blades of light like a shuttle through the warp of a loom. And we have been hitting them. Galya and I keep count. Within one week we score thirty searchlights. The sky feels safer than I have ever known it since flying as a navigator with Mara or as a pilot with Galya.

However, a few nights after we land in that beet field where we are served tea and eggs so courteously by the farmer, the weather begins to deteriorate again. Visibility is down to a few hundred meters. The fog in the Caucasus can be lethal. It reminds me of the pneumonia I once had when I was a small child. It is as if the lungs of the night are filling up. Galya is an expert navigator, but beyond our compass, our altimeter, and our wind-speed indicator, everything has to be eyesight. There's no sophisticated instrumentation on U-2s. We fly as low as we can for some sort of visual reference.

I am getting more tense by the second, and I sense Galya's growing anxiety. Her lightning-quick calculations are useless in these conditions. We'll have to find someplace to land until the fog clears. I discern a clear patch on the ground that indicates a field, but just as we enter our glide path for a landing, the fog simply evaporates. There's a lurid flash of yellow, like a livid sun in the night. I gasp as I catch sight of the black iron crosses outlined in yellow on the wings. It's a German interceptor plane, a Stuka. We can clearly see the pilot in his cockpit. His shoulders are hunched. He slides his head around in a smooth, almost reptilian movement, then grins.

"Pull up!" Galya yells.

We can't land, for if we did, we would become the perfect target. We are truly between a rock and a hard place, and utterly defenseless except for our slow speed.

But damn if we don't see him a minute later, banking a turn to come back for us. The swastika on the tail is like a brand defiling the sky. There is a burst of machine-gun fire. I hear it ping off the surface of the fuselage. Then there is the staccato of our own rear-facing machine gun. Suddenly the Stuka is gone.

There is a new quiet in the night.

"Is he gone, Galya?" I dare not turn around to see.

"I think so."

I begin a banking turn. We're going back to base. I don't think we were badly hit even with those pings off the fuselage. The ailerons are intact, that's for sure. I can see the ghostly shapes of four planes on the ground. Their props are revved and ready to go as soon as we land.

We glide in. Ironically, it is a rougher landing than the one I made when Mara was shot. As we roll to a stop, I hear Galya exhale mightily. I turn around. Her chin is bloody.

"You were hit!"

"No! You were hit," she replies.

We will laugh about this later. We have both bitten our lips bloody.

# CHAPTER 16

Last night I dreamed of Yuri. I dreamed of the touch of his hand on my face when he held it, dabbing the blood with his kerchief as I sat in the rubble in Stalingrad, watching the steamer sink just meters from the jetty. I try to remember what his fingertips felt like on my skin. Hadn't his hand cupped gently around my jawline? Didn't one finger brush my ear? Was it his trigger finger? The trigger finger of a sniper.

Yuri Vaznov's fame is spreading. He's becoming a legend, a hero. However, except for that time I told Galya a bit about him, I don't say that I know him. I need to keep those brief moments of my time with him to myself, as if they might become diluted if I share them with too many people.

I even treasure those moments of my anger when Yuri held me back from going to the jetty. I remember his words: *Your face is a bloody mess, and in this weather that blood will freeze.* That was almost six months ago—in the dead of winter. Now it's June, almost midsummer. We are, for the moment, farther north in the Caucasus and at a new airbase, so the nights are very short. Less time to bomb, more time to sleep and to dream. But dreaming is frustrating. It seems unfair that I can recall Yuri's words precisely, but not his touch.

Had I tipped my face up as if to be kissed? I have been kissed twice—no, actually, three times if you count the time with Alex. But Alex is my third cousin, so I am not sure if that counts. The others sort of counted. But they didn't stir me as the faint recollection of Yuri does. How can I be stirred by something I can hardly remember? I might be ahead on missions flown—indeed, I'm in the top ten in our regiment for summer night flights—but I'm behind on kisses, and the rest. Most of the women in the 588th have done way more than just kiss. Yana, who is not married, has a four-year-old daughter in Leningrad. And I know Tatyana has done more than kiss. She would often sneak out to be with Nikolai, her boyfriend, all through high school.

I have not seen Tatyana in nearly two months, not since we were both based on the peninsula. Each time there's been a transfer we have been sent to different airfields. I do hear through the grapevine that she is doing well and scored a really big hit recently near Krasnodar, where she wiped out a large supply convoy. Despite the tension between us, I can't help feeling proud.

The nights are growing shorter and shorter and the fighting becomes fierce. We lose several planes. When we return to base we learn that Yana has died. "Which Yana?" I ask, for there are two: Yana Zavragin and Yana Dezshnyov. Waiting for the response, I actually have to fight not to cross my fingers behind my back. What has happened to me that I'm almost praying for one Yana's death over another?

"Yana Dezshnyov," Larissa, a navigator, replies. So there is one more motherless four-year-old girl in Mother Russia. What will happen to her now? I ponder this name—the Motherland, or Rodina-mat' as it is more often called these days, and I imagine that it's supposed to reflect the spirit of collectivity in our post-czar world. But my own mother told me that the expression Mother Russia goes back to the time when the Mongols sacked the city of Kiev. I picture a big grandma in a babushka scarf spreading her skirts and gathering up hundreds of babies. We are all tiny babies, even if the men are old with bald pates and bushy beards or the women are bent with age and clutching their canes. Age does not matter. It is vulnerability that is the common denominator, and Mother Russia is there to protect us, nourish us, and defeat the Fatherland.

So why do Germans call their country the Fatherland and we are the Motherland? Curious. Maybe you need a father to win a war. But you need a mother to survive one. Is that not what happened in Stalingrad? Though millions died, a city survived. The Nazis, the "superior race," the Aryans, have finally slinked off like mongrel dogs with their tails between their legs.

The days grow hotter. The heat seems palpable, as if one

could knead it like dough, pull it out, twine it into braided loaves like those for Easter. The clouds stretch out across the nearly colorless sky like cobwebs. Flying can be hard on sunny days, for the heat in this terrain roils up like waves in a tumultuous sea. However, except for noncombat missions, we still do not fly during the day. We seek the smooth velvety air of the night that we fracture with our bombs.

I can't forget how I almost crossed my fingers when I asked which Yana had died. Is there something wrong with me? I wonder if my sister witches ever have thoughts like these. Killing from the air is easy. We see the target but not the human face behind the target. The consequences are distant. But somewhere there is undoubtedly another little four-year-old girl in Germany whose papa I have killed. Yet each night I go out with Galya. With her superb navigational skills, even in poor weather we make our hits. I know I have the most category-one target hits and am up for a medal. Not the hero medal, which is the highest, but the Order of Kutuzov, 2nd Class.

The other night we bombed a train. It must have had twenty or more cars and buckled up across the landscape like a felled behemoth. Some of the jackknifed cars scraped the night like the jagged plates on the back of a stegosaurus. It was thrilling. Am I truly becoming a witch? Have I become addicted to killing? I live now for the night.

We snatch brief periods of sleep during the seemingly endless days. I'm very suggestible, and my dreams are often prompted by scraps of conversation I hear from my fellow Night Witches. Today, the longest day of the year and the shortest night, also called the Witches' Sabbath, there's a lot of girlish chatter about boyfriends and "garland tossing." Before the war, there was a tradition of casting garlands of flowers into the river at midnight, then stripping off all one's clothes and swimming naked with one's beau. The air swells with raucous laughter as a group of mechanics, navigators, and pilots share their stories.

"I didn't intend to take off my clothes. I had worn my nightgown and the current really stripped it away. I couldn't catch it. Honestly. It floated away like a white shadow on the dark river . . . ," Oksana is saying.

"And then?" Ludmilla asks. She's a terrific pilot who flies one of the Yaks that is stationed at our airfield.

Oksana blushes madly. "Well, Cyril, a boy who never had paid attention to me, suddenly breaks through the surface of the water. All chatty."

"He caught your shadow?" Galya asks.

"Well, in a manner of speaking . . . yes . . . but he was naked too, I think."

"You think?" Galya asks.

"It was dark. No moon."

Oksana looks at us slyly, her mouth clamped shut. She will not say another word. But her good friend Ludmilla snorts. "It was about time, eh?"

Oksana still says nothing but smiles deliciously to herself and walks away.

*About time for what?* I think. I believe I'm the only virgin Night Witch. I get up and walk toward the tent. The air is crimped with heat, but it'll be smooth by tonight and the sky will embrace me, my only lover on this the shortest night of all.

I fall asleep in the heat-clotted afternoon. A kind voice threads through my dreams. *Boy,* it says. *Why are you crying?*

*I am crying because I can't get my shadow to stick on.*

I sit bolt upright on what passes for a mattress. That was not a boy speaking. It was me. But the person in the dream was not me. It was a boy huddled on the floor beneath the calendar. It was Yuri. This dream haunts me all day. What does it mean? Is it my shadow I have lost? Or is it my soul?

# CHAPTER 17

In July we're transferred to a new airfield once again, back in the Kuban region. We are bombing the western part of the Blue Line on the Kerch Peninsula, which is just across the Sea of Azov from the Taman Peninsula in the Crimea. I'm thrilled when Tatyana arrives the same day we do; the terrible things I said to her have been eating at me for too long. But I barely catch more than a glimpse of her over the next few days.

The fighting is intense from the very start. On these short nights we begin flying in three-minute intervals in order to disrupt enemy land troops. We have to vary our bombing patterns to keep the Germans from becoming too familiar with them.

The next week, Tatyana and I are both transferred to another airfield at Kursk. As we approach the airfield, we notice that there are a number of Yaks. The Yak-1 is a high-performance craft, heavily armed yet maneuverable and quite fast. It's capable of inflicting serious damage on Messerschmitts. We have barely landed, when crews run out to refuel us and an officer from the Yak regiment, Captain Iraida Ivanaov Ol'kova, comes out to brief us.

"Forty-three German aircraft are flying toward the rail junction that we're guarding. You need to take off right now and support the Yaks that are defending the junction."

We know this is hugely important. Soviet troops and ammunition have been drawn to that region in preparation for a battle that is becoming known as the Kursk Bulge. This could literally be the turn of the war. And when that turn comes, when the Nazis run west and cross into Poland, we'll be on their tails.

As we draw near, we see the Yaks attacking what seems to be a vast herd of panzer units. I come to think of this battle as a layer cake. The ground layer is composed of the panzer divisions; above them are the Yaks of the 586th; above them are the enemy aircraft; and then above them, the frosting on the cake, is us, the Night Witches, in the slipstream of the enemy, creeping up to distract or fly decoy. In just over a week the German assault is destroyed. Their dream of recovering the eastern front is wrecked. It is the largest tank battle in military history, with six thousand tanks, two million troops, and four thousand aircraft. Galya and I in our little U-2 are one of those four thousand.

Little do we suspect that barely two weeks later, our regiment will suffer its most devastating loss. Yes, the Germans are theoretically on the run, but a few stayed behind. We want them all gone, and so we intensify our air attacks as the length of the nights increases. Galya and I are soon leading the regiment in completed missions.

But as I trim off a light wind shear one night, something goes terribly wrong. There is no antiaircraft fire from the ground. Everything seems relatively silent, but then ahead of us a plane suddenly explodes.

"Jesus Christ!" Galya roars as a Russian night fighter peels away. Seconds later another craft explodes. The sky is no longer safe at all. I cut my engine to evade the enemy and plunge into a steep dive over our target. We're under six hundred meters, the lowest altitude from which it's safe to drop a bomb without serious blowback. But we do it. The shock waves buffet us, damaging our port aileron, which makes banking very difficult.

How we ever get back to the field I'll never know. As we land, I hear shouts and whoops and cries over the whir of the engine. But they're not cries of joy.

We're greeted by a grotesque scene on the runway. Dozens of people run toward us, their faces distorted with soundless screams and a wild hysterical light in their eyes.

They drag Galya and me from our cockpits. The news is almost incomprehensible. Fragments of sound, inarticulate words whip through the air. *Alina* . . . *burning* . . . *Vavara* . . . *navigator* . . . *plummeting* . . . *Stukas* . . . *a dozen* . . . *no, two dozen* . . . I smell the smoke now. A dark cloud rolls in from the west. I open my mouth to scream as their words swell with meaning. I twist my head around, frantically looking for Tatyana's plane.

The story of the attack comes out in chunks. It was massive, and within ten minutes, we lost eight members of our regiment. Four pilots and their navigators. It stands as the most horrific loss of any of the three women's regiments so far.

"Tatyana's gone?" My mouth moves around the words, but it is as if they are coming from another person.

Elena looks at me steadily. "Her plane was shot at. But Ludmilla says she saw her still flying."

"Flying where?"

"West, I think. But her rudder was hanging by threads and she was spilling fuel."

I feel Galya's hand grab my arm as I sway. All I can think of is that moment I spat on the ground as I walked away from her. I break loose from Galya's grasp and run toward the command hut. Bursting into Bershanskaya's office, I shout, "I have to go after her!" She's on a field radio with headphones and waves at me to sit down. She repeats some coordinates into the microphone before saying, "Yes, yes. Understood." She turns a switch and peels off the headphones.

"I am so sorry for your loss, comrade."

The words hit me squarely in the chest and I nearly stagger back. "I want to go."

"Go? Go where? We aren't sure if there is anyone to even rescue," she replies, her voice softer than usual.

"I don't care. If there's a chance she's out there, I'm going to find her." I rap the desk with my fist.

She reaches across the desk and grasps my hand. "Comrade Baskova, if there is a rescue mission, it will be launched from a field northwest of here, one that has Yaks. I'm sorry, but there's nothing you can do."

"I need to try. She's my *sister*."

The commander sighs. "Comrade Baskova, don't be childish. You are not going. That's final."

It's as if my entire world is sliding off its axis. The counterweight is gone, and I am slipping into a void of desolation. It occurs to me that I have always needed Tatyana to define me. I am amorphous without her, a lump of clay seeking a shape. The tears that I've been storing since I spat and turned my back on her come now. I stagger back to the shed where we sleep and throw myself on the bunk. A hot blade of morning sunlight strikes across my face. Even with my eyes closed the bright light pries at my eyelids. I press my forearm against my eyes to escape into some sort of darkness. My grief is bottomless, and I'm grieving for two of us, for I am lost as well. The person who infused me with purpose and meaning is gone. Without Tatyana I am nothing.

I fall into a strangely dreamless sleep that lasts through the remaining day and into the next night. I fight waking up. My sister's voice threads through the dregs of my sleep.

*We call it Witch's Delight when the moon is gone. More protec-*
*tion. More bombs. More kills.* When I open my eyes and look
out the small window I see it is in fact a moonless night.
There's only starlight. I hear the revving of engines. I reach
for my helmet and goggles, put on my boots, and zip my
flight jacket.

There is no time to grieve. Just time to kill.

I spend the next few weeks in a sort of daze. All I can focus
on is killing as many Germans as possible. The only moment
when the pain disappears is when I see my bomb hit a target.
In my heart of hearts I simply cannot believe that Tatyana
is dead.

I shut my eyes. I try to picture Tatyana's face. The curls of
her unruly mop of red hair dance around her heart-shaped
face like small flames. Her chin comes to a delicate point.
But I have trouble picturing her eyes. Were they green or
gray-green, or sometimes almost blue? It depended on the
light. At twilight they were gray. In the morning on a sunny
day, possibly green, and on a cloudy day, they were softly
blue. The harder I try to recall her eyes, the more difficult it
is to remember her face.

To even begin to think about her being lost, wounded, or
captured could crack my concentration while flying. There's
simply no room in the air or on the ground for such thoughts.

A few weeks later I am standing on a field in the Ukraine.
Since Kursk we had advanced steadily on the Nazis' tail.

First the city of Kharkov fell in late August. Then Smolensk. Now we are at a temporary airfield. A crisp fall breeze stirs the few unscorched wheat fields. I stand in a line stretching west to east. At the head of the line is our commander, Yevdokiya Bershanskaya. She is one of those women with a beautifully high, clear brow that seems to endow her entire being with a sense of elegant composure. But her eyes are alert. Not simply alert but keenly observant.

I am perhaps six people down from Bershanskaya. Galya is on my left, Ludmilla on my right as a plump man makes his way down the line with his aide-de-camp. Before I know it he is in front of me. His large face reminds me of a mushroom. And it seems that he has a tiny baby mushroom growing on the left side of his nose. I find this little bubble of flesh distracting. I should be used to this, as I've seen Nikita Khrushchev's picture in the newspaper numerous times. He is quite short. I'm at least ten centimeters taller. Khrushchev is commissar of the Communist party in the Ukraine. He serves as a link between Stalin and his generals on the western front, which is why he's here today. On the recommendation of General Georgy Konstantinovich Zhukov, our regiment is to receive its new and official designation. Because of our heroic actions in the Taman Peninsula, we will be known as the Forty-Sixth Taman Guards Night Bomber Regiment. We are now officially heroes of the Soviet Union.

"*Moi pozdravleniia*, comrade." Commissar Khrushchev pronounces his congratulations as he appends the medal to my left lapel. It's a round disk suspended from a red-and-blue ribbon. In the center of the disk is a hammer and sickle. The commissar's expression is somber, but it cracks suddenly with a smile, revealing teeth that are yellow and chunky. There's a gap between the two front ones that makes him appear almost feral. Nikita Sergeyevich Khrushchev implemented the Great Purge of 1934 that led to the Moscow trials that sent hundreds of thousands of Ukrainians to the gulag. "He's nothing but a criminal!" my father would say every time he saw his picture in the paper, though my mother was quick to hush him.

But the people of the Ukraine have long memories. They hold grudges. As soon as the Germans invaded in 1941, they formed the 118th Schutzmannschaft Battalion, an auxiliary police force that had more than five hundred Ukrainian volunteers. They helped the Nazis annihilate countless villages in the Ukraine and Belarus and were enthusiastic participants in the massacre of Jews in Babi Yar. Now they are on the run, and in his opening remarks, Khrushchev touts how the Red Army will ferret out every single one of these collaborators. Of course he himself was responsible for creating these collaborators when he joined Stalin in implementing the purges.

So now I am shaking hands, and a plump hand it is, with a criminal who has just pinned a medal on me.

Following the ceremony, Commander Bershanskaya explains to us the task at hand. We are to penetrate farther into the

Ukraine as the Nazis flee to the west. I'm not sure what kind of a welcome we'll get. I mean, even here at the award ceremony, there are several Ukrainian functionaries. Do I imagine that there's a flash of deep hatred every time they look at Comrade Khrushchev?

I squash the flicker of excitement that's sparked when I learn we're heading west—toward Tatyana's last known location. Over the past few weeks, I've forced myself to accept the worst. I will not even allow myself to indulge in any hope that she might have survived a crash. For hope is a terrible distraction.

# CHAPTER 18

*"Bozhe moi!"* Galya exclaims as we fly over the new airbase. "They call this temporary! *Oh my God.*"

The base is certainly impressive. It was originally built by the Nazis, and they actually have real landing lights on the airstrip, which is paved! How often have Galya and I done our approach with no lights at all, or with just the tiny glow of a ground person's cigarette.

"Can you remember how to do it with lights and strip marks?" Galya chuckles.

"I'll try."

As our wheels touch the ground I notice a short man strutting out onto the field. There's something about his walk that fills me with apprehension. He radiates a certain irascibility and arrogance. Bad combination. I see from the flat hat and the encrustations of gold braid that he is a general.

Galya and I climb down from the plane.

"Girlies!" he thunders. "They send me girlies." So much for our medals declaring us heroes of the Soviet Union.

"They keep sending me girlies." I look around. There are a lot of Soviet fighter planes here. A sprinkling of Yaks.

"We are the Forty-Sixth Taman Guard Night Bombers," I say, lifting my chin. If I'd had a bomb I would have dropped it on him. How dare he speak to us this way! But before I have time to say anything impertinent, I spot Yevdokiya Bershanskaya, marching out onto the field. She comes up to the general and touches his elbow lightly. No salute. Nothing. It's a joke among us that Commander Bershanskaya knows nothing of basic military protocol and discipline.

"Quite enough of this," she says calmly.

"Of what? What do you mean—women?" The little general almost spits the words.

Bershanskaya's green eyes burn. "Get used to us. We are women and we are proud of that. Indeed, that is the motto of our regiment. We've flown over eighteen thousand missions. We have dropped a total of twenty-five thousand tons of bombs on invading German armies. Do I need to go on? Let's make a deal. You shut up about my 'girlies' and I'll shut up about your boyos, one of whom just flew his Su-6 smack into a mountainside the clearest day we've had this autumn."

He sneers. "What are you accusing me of?"

"I'm accusing you of having an astonishing lack of vision. The Motherland knows how to use her women to the best advantage. It is only the Fatherland that squanders its female talent."

Her gaze remains level and the miserable little general seems to shrivel before our eyes. I suppress a smile of satisfaction.

"What a toad's ass," I hear Galya mutter. "Come on, let's see if this place is as first class on the ground as it looks from the air. What I wouldn't give for a good lice-free mattress."

This airbase is to be the home for our regiment and the 586th, the fighter aviation regiment that flies the Yaks. The 586th had been completely female, but a new male squadron was added recently. Apparently the general who gave us such a nasty welcome is responsible for this and wanted more male fliers. His goal isn't just to integrate the three different female regiments but to eliminate all the women fliers. But I doubt he'll have much success with our regiment. Bershanskaya will not hear of it. And what Bershanskaya wants, she gets. The entire military has profound regard for her and her innovations, from her two-plane bombing tactic to the training procedures that enabled our regiment to become one of the top-performing units in the Soviet military. It is not easy for the generals to say no to Bershanskaya.

A few days later, we're moved to another auxiliary airfield twenty kilometers closer to the front lines in Belorussia. The food is terrible, the beds lumpy, and it seems as if the surrounding countryside specializes in growing mud rather than grass. Taking off is a bit precarious, and we spend our first four days unloading sandbags to try to achieve a semblance of a runway. But once we are out of the mud and into the sky and the ever-lengthening nights, things begin to feel right to us.

One cannot speak of feeling happy or pleased or even satisfied. It is war, after all. I have lost my mother. I have no idea where my sister or my father are. I am increasingly haunted by the disappearance of Tatyana. After the fighting in the region quieted down, after the Germans retreated, the squadron commander sent in a search team, but no wreckage was sighted. Some witnesses claimed they saw her navigator fall from the plane. Others thought they heard an explosion and saw the plane falling down in flames.

Many times, I've flown over the spot where she was last spotted, but I've never seen a trace of her.

Could Tatyana have survived? If the Germans captured her and if the war ever ends, could she return to Russia? Unfortunately there is always risk in returning. That was why Mama never talked about Papa returning. Stalin believes that in Hitler's camps there are no prisoners of war, only Russian traitors. Surrender, even if one is wounded, is considered a criminal act. There are all sorts of rumors about Stalin's treatment of his own son Yakov. One story says that he was captured by the Germans, who offered to exchange Yakov for a German field marshal who'd been wounded and taken prisoner. Stalin apparently replied, "I will not trade a marshal for a lieutenant." So it's hard for me to imagine either Tatyana or Papa returning to Russia after the war if they have been captured. In Stalin's mind, "true patriots" would not permit themselves to be captured, but would have fled east to the Urals.

Such questions torment me, but I can't let them distract me. A moment's distraction in the cockpit means death. Death not just for me but for my trusted navigator—and now friend—Galya. All one can do in a situation like this is try to push the torment into the deepest, darkest corner of one's mind. You hope that the grief will begin to atrophy like a limb that shrivels from lack of use. You compensate somehow. You limp but you still move. And most importantly, you still fly.

# PART THREE

# CHAPTER 19

Our temporary airfield is in a clearing in a forest. The gathering mists grow denser and hang from the boughs like the beards of old men. The trees stand like sentries in a ghostly silence, but sometimes, I swear I hear a murmuring.

It's unclear if our airfield is in Belorussia or the Ukraine. Half the locals speak a dialect; the others speak something else. No one speaks Yiddish. The Nazis began killing Russian Jews three years ago in Babi Yar near Kiev. A hundred and fifty thousand massacred. There are rumors that a few months ago an even larger massacre took place in Poland. And we are a scant fifty kilometers from the Polish border. There is talk that many of the locals collaborated with the Nazis and helped round up the Jews. Starved by Stalin, their last shreds of humanity have withered with their flesh. And now with the Nazis in retreat, Ukraine's last hope for independence is shattered. So this is truly a no-man's-land.

The Red Army is pushing as hard as it can and we are part of that push. Our mission is to bomb any enemy supplies and clear the way for our troops. We moved in so quickly, we're warned to take pistols with us when we go into the woods to do our business, as enemy soldiers are still lurking.

When we are not flying, we pore over maps with our navigators, trying to figure out not where we are geographically but politically. As we push west, the front becomes sketchier. It reminds me in some ways of Stalingrad, where in a six-hour time period the central railroad station was taken alternately by the Red Army and the German army fourteen times. One day we hear of the Nazis taking Korosten near Kiev, and the next day the Red Army under Nikolai Fyodorovich Vatutin has recaptured it, and then, shockingly, comes the news of his assassination by the Ukrainian Insurgent Army.

One day as we are studying the maps I hear talk of a sniper.

"Yuri Vaznov?" I ask excitedly.

"No!" Galya says. "Roza Shanina." Roza Shanina has risen to sudden fame in the last few months as part of an all-female sniper platoon. She quickly racked up so many hits that she was recently awarded the Order of Glory, 3rd Class. She's the first servicewoman on the Belorussian Front to receive that distinction, and her picture is on the front page of the *Unichtozhim vraga*.

"You know"—Galya turns to the other girls—"Valya spent a romantic night with Yuri Vaznov."

"Really?" someone says as they all giggle.

Their laughter is harmless, but still I feel my face crumpling as the memory I tried to keep hidden away comes rushing back. Tears begin to spill from my eyes. I jump up and face the girls. Galya immediately senses that she has said something wrong.

"The so-called romantic night I spent with Yuri was the night my mother was murdered by a Nazi sniper. Yuri killed that sniper and sought refuge in our apartment building. I had passed out. When I awoke he was there."

"Oh, Valya," Galya says softly. "I'm sorry. You never told me the whole story. You just said he was handsome and very nice to you. I never knew the part about your mother." She is clearly distraught.

"What does it matter?" I reply flatly, and stomp off into the woods to piss.

I am squatting down in a thicket of ferns when I hear the crunch of boots behind me. I quickly draw my pistol from the holster but I see it's only Galya. She squats down beside me and starts to utter an apology when I see her face freeze. I follow her gaze. Beneath what I assumed to be a huge tangle of brambles, I detect a webbing. From it springs all matter of forest materials, and beneath that is the hulking form of a panzer. We look around, our eyes adjusting quickly to the dim green light of the deep forest. There are at least a half dozen other such tanks exquisitely camouflaged, and here we are with our pants down. We are almost nose-to-nose with these iron beasts that are hunkered down in the woods with their thick armor and bristling with guns.

Has anyone heard us? Quietly we pull up our pants and tiptoe back to the airfield. We both have the same thought. Our aircraft are all short on fuel. We have been waiting to be resupplied, but that is precisely what the tanks are waiting for. That's when they will strike: When the supply convoy approaches with fuel and parachutes and food. We have no choice but to leave immediately.

We race to our squadron commander, and in less than five minutes we have all taken off.

It is an absurd situation, I think as we climb into a blue sky furrowed with low clouds. Our small squadron encircled by a dozen panzer tanks while those same tanks are surrounded by the ever-tightening noose of the Red Army. I am in the midst of making a fifty-degree drift correction, as the wind is increasing, when suddenly Galya's voice rasps in my headphones. "Bear ninety point oh one south."

"What?" She is giving me reciprocal coordinates that would turn us back to where we came from.

"I marked it," she says.

"You marked what?" I ask.

"Where the panzers are," Galya says irritably.

"The panzers in the woods?"

"Yeah, you think I was just pissing out there? Come on. Let's blow these tanks to hell." I hear the excitement in Galya's voice.

"But we're short on fuel, Galya."

"Climb higher. We'll burn less fuel. Not only that but the clouds will be our camouflage. Better than theirs."

"Seriously?"

"Come on, let's do it!"

So I pull back on the stick, and our nose begins to point up like a dog sniffing for prey. But we are sniffing for cloud cover. Once we are tucked safely into a billowing bank, I breathe a sigh of relief, then say, "These birds are not supposed to fly on nonexistent instrumentation. How are you going to navigate, Galya?"

"Don't worry," Galya says casually, as if she were strolling through a park hoping for an ice-cream vendor. Then she gives me a steady stream of compass bearings—turn east bearing eighty-five; now angle down, five degrees west. I feel as if I have wandered into the clockworks of a human calculator. She spins off the numbers and I just fly the plane accordingly. "Crab fifteen degrees off the wind." How she ever calculates the drift correction with these clouds covering the ground and any visible object I'll never know. "Approaching target . . . duck out!"

I dive out of the cloud cover. She pulls the latch of the bomb. There is the sound of a massive explosion, but the plane just jiggles slightly. We have never dropped a bomb from this high an altitude.

"Music to my ears!" Galya shouts. "The sound of panzers dying." I pull back on the stick again and we race for the clouds. Behind us there are more explosions as the rest of the tanks erupt in flames. The panzers and especially the huge ones called Tigers carry enormous fuel loads. Soon a forest fire is raging. The flames tear at the sky behind us.

The fuel-tank needle is jittering over the *E*. Within seconds it is on *E* and the engine dies. I put the nose down and we begin a long glide into the next airfield.

"We thought they got you!" Ludmilla cries, running out to meet our plane.

"No!" Galya booms jubilantly. "We got them!"

"*You* got them, Galya," I say.

"I couldn't have done it without your flying."

"I couldn't have done it if you hadn't taken that compass bearing when we were in the woods."

"What?" Ludmilla asks. Others have now gathered around.

Galya's broad, freckled face breaks into a toothy smile. "Moral of the story: Never take a shit in the woods without your compass. No telling what kind of turds you'll bump into."

# CHAPTER 20

We keep pushing west. Our parachutes have finally arrived, but I'm not sure what use they could be. It would be like jumping from the frying pan into the fire, for our task is to prevent enemy bombers from taking off. I delight in every successful bombing raid, and in every westward kilometer we gain. But at the same time I worry. I know the Germans keep prisoners of war near our target sites. Might I be blowing up my own sister? I can't let myself be distracted, but the notion of rescuing Tatyana remains like a bright filament threading through my mind.

Galya and I are charged with mapping a course for the Yak regiment with the heavy firepower to follow. We drop incendiaries, which create small fires indicating the location of the enemy airfield so that Yak bombers can swoop in after us with the really big bombs and set the airfields and the planes on fire. We have to fly low, and directly above the enemy airstrip. As soon as we drop these flare bombs we become vulnerable. A terrible silence follows as their searchlights rake the sky. How long will it take the enemy ground fire to react? I've never had to concentrate so hard, and my whole body becomes a distillation of nerves. I feel as if Galya and I are one inseparable vascular system for pumping adrenaline.

One night we are well past the enemy airstrip, when I smell petrol in the cockpit. Our fuel line must have been hit. But how? A sudden fog envelops us. "Were we hit?" I yell through the intercom. No answer. "Galya, give me some bearings!" Nothing. "Galya, for Chrissake . . ." My human calculator who spews numbers at lightning speed is silent. I'm flying blind now. I touch my scarf, Mara's scarf. We slide into a stall as we lose speed and altitude. I hear the tops of trees thrashing at the fuselage and turn around in my seat.

There is no Galya. She has vanished. There is only a big hole where her seat was. Cold terror engulfs me, and my breath locks in my throat. It's as if God or the Devil has played a terrible trick. Has she been torn out of the plane— seat and all? Did she have time to open her chute? Did she plummet into the flames from the Yaks' bombing of the airstrip? The plane is now shaking. I have lost all control. That is my last thought before I feel a jolt of pain and everything turns black.

The darkness that's enveloped me begins to fray. Shapes emerge from the shadows, and I'm afraid of what I might see, or not see. *My God*, I think. *Am I in a Russian folktale?* A plump figure swathed in colorful shawls sits in a rocking chair. She is wearing a *kokoshnik*, or hen's hat, that arches over her head. Two long, fat iron-gray braids fall on each side of her plump face. Her cheeks, like two rosy apples, nearly obscure her tiny mouth. Her chin is also as round as a robust little crab apple.

"So you wake up?" She has a thick Ukrainian accent. I am in a bed in a small room. My leg feels strange. I try to move it under the covers.

"Did I . . . ?"

She shakes her head. "No. Not broken. But I fix it in splint anyway."

"Thank you . . . uh." I put my hand to my neck. The scarf, Mara's scarf, is still there. "How long have I been here?"

"Not long." She shrugs. It seems a strange way to answer. I look out the small window. It's bright sunshine, suggesting midday. But I crashed at night. "You would like some soup?"

"Oh, yes. That would be nice." I start to move.

"Do not try to walk yet. That leg is very bruised and with the splint."

She gets up from the chair. I watch her as she walks out of the room. Her gait is peculiar. I try to decide if one would describe it as a waddle or a toddle. Silly question. I wonder if she lives alone, and if she does, how she moved me from the plane to here.

And my plane? Not a silly question. Is it in smithereens? Did it burn? The frightening moments replay in my head: The smell of fuel filling the cockpit. The stall. The fog. The sound of the treetops scraping the fuselage. And then my mind explodes with the worst image of all. The nothingness when I turned to look for Galya and saw only the hole in the cockpit where she had sat in the navigator's seat. By the time the woman returns with the soup I am leaking tears. She sets down the tray and puts her arm around my shoulders. "Here, here," she says. I am making odd sounds. Funny little hiccups and gurgles. Sounds that I don't even recognize as coming from me. "Is . . . is . . . or did you . . ." I am not sure how to say this. The words fly away like a flock of startled birds. Finally I gasp, "Did you find my navigator?"

"Navigator?" She puts her hand to her ear. "Say again, I am a tad deaf." I soon learn it's more than a tad. I constantly have to repeat words or questions.

"My . . . my friend . . . Galya." I cannot bring myself to say the word *body*. Galya cannot be a body. There have been too many bodies.

She opens her dark eyes wide. "No, no. Just you. I find you."

"And you brought me here . . . here into your house."

"Eh?" She cups her ear again.

"You brought me here to your house."

"Yes."

"But how? Did you drag me all by yourself?" A shadow seems to cross her face. She nods decisively. "You live here alone?" Again she nods. The little crab-apple chin bobs up and down. "But how did you do it all by yourself?"

"I put you on the sledge and my donkey drags you."

"Oh . . . oh, yes. I see. But you are sure there was no other person."

"Not your friend. No one," she says firmly.

"And the plane?"

"It's in worse shape than you are. Don't worry about the plane. Now, eat your soup. Be a good girl. Eat."

As I eat, I look around the bedroom. There are yellowed curtains with a crocheted fringe, and a bad painting of a sunflower. The quilt on my bed is a traditional block design with a different flower in each block. There is a small icon of, I believe, the archangel Mikhail, for he is lifting a sword. Mikhail is the patron saint of war and of the police.

I follow her advice and rest for a few days. The old lady's name is Rufina. She shares her food with me, and teaches me how to make *khrustiki*, or "ears," the Ukrainian pastry that's so light and crunchy. She never tells me much about her family. There are some pictures around, but I don't want to ask. Undoubtedly she, like me, has lost loved ones in this war. Perhaps because I am not flying half a dozen raids a day, perhaps because for the first time I have time on my hands, I think more and more about Tatyana. I survived the crash, so perhaps Tatyana did as well. Maybe she too is being cared for in a cozy farmhouse eating dumplings and *khrustyki*. Maybe . . . maybe . . . she is not broken into pieces, her limbs twisted and charred.

As my leg heals and I'm able to get around better, I start taking short walks. But Rufina is adamant that I not "overdo it." I keep mostly to the barnyard. I enjoy picking up the eggs from the henhouse. There's one hen who is quite a character. She's taken a fancy to me. If I sit down on the board that serves as the makeshift bench, she will hop up onto my lap. This gives Rufina a good laugh.

"I am jealous," she says to me each time the hen settles on my lap. "Why you and not me? I've been so good to that hen. Could have put her in a stew months ago."

The word *months* triggers something in my mind. How long have I been here? We seem so far from the front. On that last bombing raid we were about fifty kilometers west of Belarus in Minsk. But I have no idea where I crashed. I am hesitant to ask if Rufina has heard any news about the war. I tried once and it was as if her face turned to stone. I can't say I blame her. The little house seems idyllic, nestled among rolling green hills. She receives food from the collective farm, the *artel*, near her, but she is permitted to keep a few chickens for herself as long as she gives half of the eggs to the collective. She also has a small vegetable garden, two-thirds of which she must also give to the *artel*. I have seen no trace of the donkey that dragged the sledge with me unconscious up to her house, but I assume that it was on loan to her for the day from the *artel*. When I get stronger and can walk farther, I plan to set out to see my plane, or what's left of it.

Since I have been here no one has visited Rufina.

I have begun to help her with chores around the house and in the vegetable garden. I clean out the chicken coops and weed the garden. I even climb a ladder to nail a loose shutter for her. She is very grateful. But she still doesn't want me to walk very far. One day when I mention that I feel fit enough to hike to where my plane crashed, she becomes very upset.

"It is only across the meadow there at the edge of the forest. I can do it. My leg is so much stronger now," I say.

"The meadow is full of holes and turns marshy with swales. It is not easy. And the forest is full of wolves. You hear them howling at night, don't you?"

I shake my head. I haven't heard a wolf howling since I have been here. "But, Rufina," I argue, "you walked across the meadow and back, dragging me on a sledge pulled by a donkey."

"Donkeys are sure-footed."

"What about the wolves? They didn't eat you."

"I am a tough old lady. Nothing juicy." Her eyes turn misty. "I feed you. I tend to you. I do not want you injuring yourself again. That is too much for an old woman. You know doctors don't grow on trees around here."

I promise I won't walk to the plane, but a strange unease begins to set in. Our jokes about the hen become rather brittle. There are fewer cooking lessons. Rufina seems to be waiting for something, and this makes me nervous. She seems to watch me constantly. If I disappear around the corner of the chicken house, she shouts out, "Where are you, dearie?"

I look at the sky longingly. I feel trapped—trapped in this Eden where the meadows are dotted with wildflowers. I don't care if it's surrounded by a wolf-ridden forest. I am determined to go to my plane. It's the womb where I was reconceived as a fighter. I am a fighter. That is what I do. Fight.

# CHAPTER 21

I decide I'll go to the plane at night. I can tell there's a storm coming, one of the ferocious electrical storms with forks of lightning sizzling overhead, which will keep anyone in their right mind from venturing out. I know weather now. We Night Witches have learned it. We feel the heaviness in the air. We have a sixth sense for dew points, an uncanny sensitivity for air pressure and humidity and the critical moment when water begins to condense into droplets. I know weather, and tonight a storm is coming in from the east. By the time we sit down for supper, the pitter of the rain begins. When I fetch the teakettle I see Rufina yawning. "No tea for me." She yawns again. "I don't know what it is, but summer rainstorms make me sleepy."

"Would you like me to help you to bed?" I have to repeat it twice.

"Oh, yes, how kind. I am feeling especially tired tonight. You are a good girl." She pauses as if she wants to say something more but dares not. I help her from the chair and take her to her room. It is the first time I have seen her bedroom.

There is a picture of a young man on a shelf. It must be her son, for he too has the rounded little crab-apple chin. Above the picture is another icon, the archangel Mikhail. I guess that her son is named Mikhail.

Funny, I think, how such distinct traits run in families. I have a dimple in my cheek. "Very flirtatious! Just like your mother," my father used to say. "It certainly caught my attention the first time your mother made eyes at me."

"I didn't make eyes at you, Peter. You chased me, if you recall," my mother had said.

"I didn't chase you. I strolled alongside of you casually. Like a Parisian boulevardier."

"What's that?" I had asked.

"A man about town," Papa said.

"Man about Paris. Your father was just back from Paris."

These fragments of conversation float through my mind as I help Rufina take off her shoes.

"Thank you, dear. I can do the rest."

The rain is pounding down now, and a fork of lightning snags the darkness, illuminating the bedroom for a split second. Rufina lies down, and soon her snoring reverberates throughout the small house.

I have it all planned out. I'm not going to wear my clothes, but will go in my undergarments. If she finds wet clothes she'll know. I also plan to go barefoot. I don't want a trace of mud on my boots.

I creep out of the house and shut the door as quietly as I can, and then tear out through the barnyard. There's a patch of fluffy white directly in my path. I can't believe it. That stupid hen! What is she doing out on such a night? I stare at her fiercely. *"Quiet,"* I hiss. She backs off, appalled that her best friend in all the Ukraine would do such a thing. I dodge around her, for she seems stuck to the ground. Another two seconds and I'm out of the barnyard, racing toward the meadow. The sky is splintered with lightning. I could be struck, electrocuted, but this doesn't deter me. I have flown through flak storms, woven through the searing beams of Nazi searchlights.

The meadow has become a wind-whipped sea of grass that slashes at my bare legs. At the far edge I can see the forest line, and between the cracks of thunder I hear the creaks and groans of the timber. I stop to catch my breath and open my eyes wide. Through the rain-torn night, straight ahead at the edge of the meadow, I see the hulk of my craft. The fragment of the number three is clear on the tail, and though the fuselage is scorched, I can see the red star. One of the two blades of the propeller is driven into the ground, the other sticks up jauntily, as if giving a crisp salute. I rush to the little craft. I want to hug it. I fold my arms around the prop. Tears stream from my face. I'm crying—crying for the plane, crying for Galya, crying for Mara, crying for Tatyana. Crying for all the broken things in my life.

I crawl through the wreckage and find the compass. Miraculously, it's still working. My goggles and leather flight cap have been left on the seat. Rufina must have removed the goggles and flight cap from my head. I continue to look around the plane's interior. I don't find our navigation charts, and assume they must have fallen out of the plane when Galya fell. She was flying with the charts on her lap. I find our canteens, which are still filled with water. Not a dent in them. But, oddly, the chocolate is missing. We always flew with chocolate. How did the canteens survive but the chocolate disappear? Wolves? *Do wolves like chocolate?* I wonder.

I sit on the crumpled wing of the plane. The rain momentarily ceases and the clouds scuttle off, revealing a black pool with three shining stars. It must be the belt of Orion. I know those stars. We learned their names together, Tatyana and I—Alnitak, Alnilam, and Mintaka. As I look up at the three stars glittering in the patch of cleared sky, they seem to pulse, to breathe, and it comes to me like a story whispered in the night. *She lives! Tatyana lives.* I know this. All doubt vanishes from my mind. I can feel her out there, calling to me.

The clouds begin to creep back, peeling away the pitch black until the stars are obliterated. But the image of Tatyana alive is burnished in my mind, as glittering as any star. I see her knees jackknifing up as she clears the hurdles. She is running. I hear the beat of her heart, the pounding of her feet on the track. God, can that girl run. She is uncatchable.

I sit and grasp my own knees. It begins to rain again. Clouds writhe and whorl above me, but my mind seems illuminated. Her spirit fills me. I feel emboldened and get up from the wing to continue my walk around the plane. It is almost as if Tatyana were walking with me. I can hear her voice now. *Checklist, Valya. Always the preflight checklist before a pilot takes off.* Of course, this plane is not going anywhere. The fuel tank's broken feed line snakes through the grass, there's a gaping hole in the side of the fuselage, and one broken wing. But Tatyana's voice still rings in my ear. *There's always something to learn, Valya. You are young and impatient. Impetuous. You need to be more mature about these things.*

Even in my head, her voice has the same condescending tone, but now I rejoice.

Still, my situation is dangerous. It's not the wolves in the woods that I fear, not the ones that Rufina spoke of. There are other wolves—German wolves. And a gun, my gun, is missing. There's only one person who could have it.

I know I must get back to the house. But it's hard for me to leave this poor wrecked creature, the plane that's been so loyal to me for so long.

As I walk back through the driving rain, my apprehension increases. Why would Rufina have taken the pistol? What would an old lady need with one? Did a wolf step out of the forest and threaten her once?

As I approach the house, I stand and look at its inky shadow spread across the barnyard. The house seems ominous now. Clouds rumble across the sky, and the slender limbs of two pear trees bicker in the wind. Another flash of lightning strips away the darkness, and for just a fraction of a second the world is too bright. The little house stands like a weirdly mute shriek in the night. A warning. It is a house with too many secrets. I want to run. But what can I do? I'm standing in the middle of the Ukraine in my underwear. I have no pistol, no shoes; my plane is wrecked. I have no choice. I have to go back inside. I have to find my pistol. And in order to do this, I have to become an actor in a drama. But I'm not even sure of the plotline, let alone the ending.

When I'm inside I hear the raucous snores still issuing forth from the bedroom. I'm careful not to track in any mud, or even a blade of grass from the meadow. The next morning I come into the kitchen to find Rufina busy getting the fire started in the wood-burning stove.

"Small fire this morning. I should have gotten in more wood before that storm," she says. "It is enough for one pot of tea."

"Oh, you drink the tea," I say. "I don't need it."

"Eh?"

"I said you drink the tea; I don't need it."

"There is enough for two mugs at least, dearie." The hairs on my neck stand up a little bit when she calls me "dearie."

"It's going to be a hot one today. I'll stay cooler if I don't drink hot tea."

"Now, you know what, dearie?"

"What, Rufina?"

She shakes her finger at me. "What you just said about keeping cooler is nonsense. Quite the opposite is true, in fact. If you drink a hot drink on a summer day, in the morning . . ."

I force a smile. "My babushka told me the same thing."

"And you are going to say it is an old wives' tale."

I seem to be able to summon up a true blush. "No, I am just going to say that you remind me of my grandmother." She seems to melt a bit. What an actress I am! But the entire time I'm thinking about the pistol. Where could she have hidden it? What is she fearful I will do? I am under surveillance. And now I not only feel it in Rufina's eyes but in others that are watching me from afar. Why does no one ever come to visit her? We are like far-flung planets in another solar system, and yet there are alien eyes pressed to telescopes observing us.

It is, of course, impossible for me to search for the gun during the day. At night I make several forays around the tiny house as she snores away in her room.

The next few days grow hotter. It is a throbbing heat that seems to glaze the air. We have dug a great number of the little thin-skinned potatoes that the Ukraine is so famous for. Suddenly big sledgehammer clouds swim across the sky. Everything turns dark and raindrops the size of cherries begin to splash down on us.

"Quick!" Rufina shouts. "To the root cellar with the potatoes." Even I know that these potatoes are delicate. They can't endure being wet except in a pot of boiling water for thirty seconds.

I pick up our baskets and begin to run. She follows with a dozen or more potatoes in her skirt. I set down the baskets to swing open the root cellar door. "Over there in the corner." She points. "Spread them out. Right on the floor. They mustn't be in piles or they'll rot."

I do as she says, and before I know it she has grabbed the baskets and gone for another load. "I can do that," I say. "You needn't get all wet."

"We're both all wet already, dearie. But sure. You get wet. I'll let you do that."

I am back within a couple of minutes. She takes the basket from me. "Now go upstairs and change." There's a strange urgency in her voice.

As I turn to go, my eye falls on something chilling. The corner of the cloth that I spread the potatoes on is turned up just a bit, and I recognize the pattern. It's not a random piece of canvas. It is a *zeltbahn* cape. A *Nazi zeltbahn* cape. I recognize the camouflage pattern. I saw it in Stalingrad. Dread and clarity wash over me in equal measure. I know why Rufina has been keeping me here. And I have a strong suspicion about where she hid my pistol. My heart is beating so hard I think that even in her deafness Rufina can hear it. I am thankful for the dim light, for I know I am turning white with rage.

*     *     *

Rufina is exhausted from the heat of the day and the work. By suppertime she can hardly move. She pours herself a tot of vodka and offers me some. I pretend to drink it. Before the sun sets she is snoring away in her bedroom. "Dearie, you are a good girl. Too good . . . ," she mumbles as she drops off to sleep.

Twilight is thickening as I make my way to the root cellar. I've taken a small candle with me, but before I light it I let my eyes adjust to the darkness. I vow not to light the candle until I need to. As I search, I wonder if Rufina even thought of the danger of letting me help her bring the potatoes into the cellar. Even if the gun is not here, there is the *zeltbahn*. That, of course, is the corner that I go to first. It is indeed a true *zeltbahn* cape. There's a name on a patch: Mikhail Popischev, SMSCH 118. This confirms it. Her son, Mikhail, is a member of the dreaded 118th Schutzmannschaft Battalion, an auxiliary Ukrainian police force, known collaborators with Nazis. I am in the belly of the beast here. I have unwittingly surrendered to the enemy and committed a criminal act. According to Stalin, there are no prisoners of war. Only Russian traitors.

# CHAPTER 22

I never even have to light the candle. It takes me less than five minutes to find the pistol and the few last pieces of chocolate. I leave the chocolate and take the pistol, fashioning a kind of holster from a bag of old rags Rufina kept. Luckily my clothes are bulky and I plan to wear the pistol constantly. My plan is to leave tomorrow. I don't know where I will go, but I do have a compass. I brought it back the night I went to the plane and tucked it into a tree stump at the edge of the field so I could retrieve it later. But I'm not quite sure what to do until then. Every minute of the next day I try to keep up the act, joking with Rufina about my babushka, humming a little tune, and trying to appear cheerful all while the pistol bumps softly against my stomach. I keep thinking that her son, Mikhail, will show up any minute. I swear someone is watching me. I just feel it.

Everything seems to go well until just before suppertime. I come into the kitchen. Rufina's back is toward me as she cooks, but I can tell from her posture that something is wrong. Water is boiling and in a bright green bowl are a dozen or so of the little potatoes!

She's been to the root cellar! She's discovered my theft.

We eat dinner in near silence. My jokes fall flat. Rufina does not have a gift for improvisation under stress. She begins to yawn elaborately. Too elaborately. She makes an excuse for going to bed as soon as it is dark.

"Yes, I'm tired too," I say. She looks at me narrowly. There is a pinched darkness in her eyes. "Let's have some tea. Then we'll go to sleep." I get up to get the kettle going.

"No, let me fix it," she says in a very insistent tone.

She's going to poison me. Or drug me at best. I am Gretel without Hansel and I have stumbled into the witch's candy-encrusted house.

"Dearie, would you go out to the henhouse and fetch an extra egg? I think I will mix one in with my tea. It is strengthening, you know."

"Another old wives' tale?" I joke. She tries to laugh but it doesn't work. Only a harsh gargle noise issues forth.

I go to fetch the egg. I have been in much worse danger, I tell myself. I can fly out of this. I have the pistol strapped beneath my skirts. I could simply come back and shoot her. But would that be the end of it? There are those eyes out there, watching me. I feel them. There are not wolves in the woods but the police, the Schutzmannschaft, and if they hear the crack of a pistol shot . . . well, I dare not think what would happen. The Schutzmannschaft will come for me the way they came for the Jews and marched them to the ravine at Babi Yar to be massacred. I can hear those mute screams as the dusk settles over the hills like a shroud.

I have to get out. But night hasn't fallen. If I run now they will chase me. Why are they waiting? I realize I am trembling. I carry Mara's scarf in my pocket and touch it, as I would touch it when I was flying for courage. My brain clears and I return to the kitchen and give her the egg.

"Thank you," she mutters but barely looks at me. Her hands tremble as she cracks the egg into her mug. A minute later she comes to the table with both mugs. Now her eyes are fastened on me. How will I do this? I begin with a little sip. While the cup is still at my lips, I dip my chin and let the liquid spill into my scarf. Will she notice? While she bends over her cup I raise mine again. This time I take a larger "swallow." She has put a lot of sugar in the tea. Again I let it dribble into the scarf. Perhaps it's not poison but a sleeping draft.

Then the best thing happens. Rufina gets up and bumps the table, which is quite rickety. Both mugs tip over and spill the remains of their contents. She emits a gasp of distress, followed by a muttered curse.

"Never mind," I say quickly, "I've had enough," and then yawn. There is a flicker of light in her eyes. *Sleeping medicine*, I think. But why does she want me to sleep? Why should I be asleep when the Schutzmannschaft come, when her son the archangel arrives to deliver me? For I'm sure that is her plan.

By the time I crawl into bed, dusk has thickened to darkness. I grasp the barrel of the pistol. It grows warm in my hand. I hear a creak in the floorboards outside my door. A liquid shadow slides beneath the door as it opens, then spills across the moon-washed wall, creating the silhouette of a lifted ax. I spring from the bed and, holding the pistol with both hands, cock the trigger. The scent of chocolate swirls through the air.

"*No!*" I say.

We stand scant meters apart. I've never come face-to-face with my victims. Never until this moment. And again the smell of chocolate seeps into my nostrils. *My* chocolate. I feel the undertow of an overwhelming fatigue pulling me down. I cannot kill anymore. The gun wobbles in my hand, and then I hear a deafening crack. Rufina looks at me in complete shock. A chunk of her head falls on the floor as she crumples.

I drop the gun to my side. My finger is still on the trigger and yet there was no recoil. I didn't fire the shot. As I stand, staring in horror, a young woman emerges from the shadows and jumps over Rufina's fallen body.

"Come on! We're out of here," she hisses at me. She's holding a pistol, and slung across her back is a Mosin-Nagant sniper rifle.

Even in the dim light, I recognize the sniper Roza Shanina. She's one of the most beautiful women I have ever seen. Her strawberry-blond hair is arranged primly in a school-marmish bun. A galaxy of pale freckles is sprinkled across her cheeks. She grabs me by the elbow and steers me out of the room. I twist around to look at the body of Rufina.

"Don't look back! Never look back."

We are racing across the field. Roza swerves right, toward the road that cuts through a pasture. There ahead of us is a Yak, and standing by the propeller is Galya! It's such a beautiful sight, I can barely believe it. She takes off her flight cap and waves it joyously.

I break away from Roza and dash into Galya's arms.

"You're alive! How is that possible?" I am sobbing.

"No time for explanations. In you go. Be my navigator for just this flight," Galya says.

Within two minutes, we are up in the air. Roza and I are squashed into the rear cockpit. The sky folds around me. The stars sing. My pant legs are splattered with blood. Galya hands me the coordinates for the flight plan.

"Where are we going?"

"Poland."

The front has moved to Poland already? Galya explains that the Red Army has been extraordinarily successful. We have pushed the Nazis west. The entire front of the war has moved. The Germans are out of the Motherland.

Roza was right. We can't look back. Just ahead.

I will never see Roza again. She was brought in by Commander Bershanskaya when a surveillance plane spotted my crashed aircraft. And it's odd, but after that night I never dream of Yuri again. I think of him but I never dream of him. He has dissolved like a vapor on a sunny morning.

# CHAPTER 23

Galya's hands are a few inches apart. She is bringing them together slowly. I have seen half a dozen of my fellow Night Witches make this same gesture as they describe what has happened since I crashed. There's been a major shift in the war. The Allies have managed to surround the Germans and are preparing for a final push.

So much has happened since my crash, I might as well have been on another planet, in another solar system. "You see, from the west and the east we are squeezing them!" she exclaims, and claps her hands together. How Galya survived that crash is another story. Somehow she fell out of that plane in the flight seat and managed to open her parachute. She was quickly picked up by men from a Soviet infantry unit.

"Tell me one more time, Galya, how all this happened. About the Allies landing on the beaches in France. When was it exactly?"

"June sixth. First the paratroopers went in, thirteen thousand of them."

My eyes widen. "Thirteen thousand! That's a lot of Geronimos."

"They probably weren't shouting." Galya laughs. "They wanted to sneak in before dawn."

"What next?" I lean in, enthralled as a child listening to a favorite story.

"The assault by sea. That was the most incredible part. Twenty-one thousand infantry landing on Utah Beach. They cleared out the Germans there and within hours had penetrated nearly eleven kilometers into France."

"Incredible!" I say.

"Inspiring. It was like a jolt of adrenaline into our troops. Then we started moving west on the tails of the Nazis while the Allies started to move east." She raises her hands again. "We're squeezing them, Valya. We're going to strangle the Nazis."

"And it was in Lublin where they discovered a concentration camp and all those horrible . . . horrible . . ." I trail off. I cannot fathom what I've been hearing about these camps—the atrocities that the Nazis committed.

This morning, we are awaiting our commander, Yevdokiya Bershanskaya, in a tent at a temporary airfield near Krosno in southern Poland. A map of the surrounding area has been set up, and we all stare at it, wondering about our next mission.

Bershanskaya strides into the room. Her green eyes are

calm and steady, her shoulders squared. In some people the weariness of war is apparent, but not in Bershanskaya. Not a gray hair. Not a wrinkle in her tranquil brow. She flashes us a warm smile and takes up a pointer.

"Ladies, I give you the Vistula River, the longest river in Poland. Our focus is here." She taps the map near the city of L'viv. "We are determined to hold it. That means protecting the Vistula bridgeheads. We have close to forty antitank artillery forces there repulsing the counterattacks of the German armored forces. *Our* job is to make sure the Red Army can do *its* job and defend the bridgeheads in this area." She taps the map, indicating the cities of Magnuszew and Puławy. "The other regiments will be taking care of the northern bridgeheads toward Warsaw. It is up to us and the other aviation units to protect this Ukrainian front and make sure it does not slip back into Nazi claws. Thirty-two air divisions have been assigned. So including us, the Taman Guards, we'll have the 586th Fighter Regiment and the 125th Guard Bombers. As you know, there are many men in those formerly all-female units. Only we, the Taman Guards, remain completely women. Let's show them what we can do!" We all cheer. I cheer the loudest. I am grateful to be back, grateful for the chance to fight again.

As we disperse from the meeting, Bershanskaya signals me to follow her into her quarters. When I enter, I find her leaning on the small desk with both fists planted on the top. She looks at me for several seconds before speaking. Her forehead is crinkled and a ferocious light flickers in the limpid green eyes. It is as if there is a storm gathering.

"You are very good, Valya. Over the past week, you've flown more than a dozen missions and hit extremely difficult targets every single time. Quite remarkable, especially after not flying for so long."

"Thank you," I say, my voice quavering. What is she going to tell me?

"This task we have been given, the bombing of the ammo depot, is going to be complex. As you know, the civilians in that part of the Belarusian-Polish border are not what one could call solid allies. The Schutzmannschaft is very active. Pockets of collaborators all over. Worse than where you were on that farm. Extracting you was relatively easy. I was so pleased when Galya came back with those coordinates. Ever since Operation Bagration began, getting you out was a primary objective."

She sees the astonishment in my face and continues. "Yes, I wanted you because I knew sooner or later the Red Army would be crossing the Vistula and protecting the bridgeheads would be key. It will depend almost entirely on air divisions. The Taman Guard will have forty aircraft flying. Half of our planes will be led by me. I want you to lead the other half."

Surprise and excitement course through me. "I am honored, Commander."

"That is beside the point," she says curtly, and reaches for something in her pocket. She slaps it on the desk. It is a small packet. "If you go down and survive, the Germans will capture you."

"I know there are no prisoners of war. Only traitors."

"It is worse than that," she says. "Did you hear that Stalin's son Jacob committed suicide when he heard his father denied having a son?"

I shake my head. "No, I didn't hear that. What are you trying to tell me?" My eyes fix on the packet. I know what's in it. Cyanide tablets. There have been rumors about these being issued to prevent prisoners of war from revealing secrets under torture.

"Now, listen to me carefully, Valentina." She leans across the desk, her face inches from mine. "I am not worried about you being tortured by the Nazis. I am worried about you being tortured by Joseph Stalin. I am going to tell you a dirty little secret. Does SMERSH mean anything to you?"

"Counterintelligence, right?"

"Yes; 'death to fascists' is what the acronym stands for. The SMERSH agents work hand in glove with NKVD."

"Right," I say slowly, trying to process what she is getting at.

"You see," she continues, "every time a German prison camp is liberated, these SMERSH units and NKVD officers move in to interrogate the Russian prisoners, the 'traitors' who allowed themselves to be captured. These agents are charged with evaluating the prisoners' loyalty to the Soviet Union. Stalin is paranoid. He is as bad as Hitler," she whispers hoarsely. *Oh, she has said it!* I think. She has said what none of us have dared to say out loud for years. It's why Mama never wanted to talk about Papa after he disappeared. She feared for the worst. She feared a fate much worse than death.

"Have you told the others this?"

Something seems to deflate within her. She shakes her head. "How can I hand a packet of cyanide to every single pilot and navigator and tell them what I just told you and then expect them to fly?" She pauses and looks at me. To my surprise, her eyes well with tears. "I *had* to tell you. I can't be dishonest with you and expect you to lead. You are a wing commander now. This is the terror of such responsibility."

I nod and start to leave.

"Not yet, Comrade Baskova." She points to a chair. "Please sit down. There is someone I want you to meet. Though I believe you may already know him."

"What? Who?" I ask, looking around the room.

"Comrade Vasnov, you may enter now."

My heart leaps into my throat as, from a door I never noticed in the rear of the office, Yuri steps out.

"Surprised?" he says with a small smile. I'm speechless. Once again Yuri has emerged from the vaporous mists of war. "I was going to come rescue you myself, but Roza was closer."

I remain silent as the words sink in. All those weeks when I felt so stranded, so alone, Yuri was thinking about me. "You were worried about me?" I say finally.

"Worried about a girl who's flown over five hundred bombing missions? No, not really. I know you can take care of yourself. But someone had to fetch you at some point."

"So what are you doing here now?" I ask, noticing Commander Bershanskaya glance quickly between us. I have the sense of someone watching a tennis match, but the match is too slow for her liking.

"Yuri came to deliver some important news," she said. "We have cause to believe that your sister is in one of the camps near Smolensk."

I leap from my chair. "You mean she's *alive*?"

Yuri takes a deep breath. "Roza and I infiltrated that camp less than a week ago. We picked off half a dozen guards. I saw Tatyana in one of the infirmary buildings. Roza saw her too." He rubs his forehead.

"How did you know it was my sister?"

"She looks so much like you." He reaches out and touches my hair.

"But my hair isn't red."

"No, it's gold. But it's your sister that I saw. Believe me. I had her in my crosshairs for hours, or so it seems."

His words seem to suck all the air from my lungs. "In your crosshairs? Why?"

"I was trying to take out the men guarding her and the other prisoners. Her head kept getting in the way."

"So my sister lives," I say wondrously. It seems so miraculous, it's as if I'm tasting starlight. The very starlight I saw when I sat on the wing of my crashed plane and glimpsed Orion's Belt and knew she lived. My wonder hardens into steely resolve. "I need to rescue her."

"Yes, but you must wait for the right moment," Bershanskaya says. "Remember, between you and your sister in that camp are a dozen or more bridgeheads on the Vistula River. That ammo depot must be blown up *before* you can rescue her. Those bridgeheads must be protected so the Red Army can get through. Go to the mess and get yourself some coffee and food. Your plane will be ready to fly in"— she looks at her watch—"exactly ten minutes. And be sure to keep this a secret." She glances toward the door, as if worried about eavesdroppers. "No rescue mission has been authorized. You must go and return without being caught."

I can feel the cyanide tablets in my pocket. If I don't get to Tatyana soon, she could be killed as a traitor by our own forces. I don't have a minute to lose.

"Thank you," I say to Yuri as we leave Bershanskaya's quarters. "You don't know what this means to me."

"It's a pleasure to share good news for once," he says stiffly; then his voice softens. "I hope you find her, Valya. I hope you both make it back safely."

I nod. "Would you like something to eat before you go?"

He shakes his head. "I've been gone for too long as it is. Perhaps I'll see you again, when all this is done."

"Perhaps," I say, smiling slightly at the idea of seeing Yuri when we can focus on talking—and maybe laughing—instead of killing.

He places his hand on my arm, squeezes it, and then he's gone.

Dirty little secrets have a way of spreading. There's an eerie quiet as I walk into the mess. I see everyone stealing glances toward a table in the corner. Ivan Orlyev, deputy chief of SMERSH on the Belorussian Front, is sitting with his pal from the NKVD, Anton Semenov. Suddenly my stomach is not up for food. But it's too late. I feel their eyes rake over me for clues that might betray a potential "traitor." They rise and begin making their way toward me. They remind me of cartoon characters. In my head they become Smitt and Smatt. Maybe like Mutt and Jeff, the favorites of many Russian kids.

"Comrade Baskova?" Orlyev asks. I nod. "I understand that you are to function as a wing commander in the defense of the bridgeheads of Vistula."

I hate the way this man speaks. *Function?* As if I am a cog in a piece of machinery. "Yes, sir."

"And I understand that your sister went down somewhere in Kursk."

My stomach clenches. "Yes, sir."

"Never found, eh?"

"Never found, sir."

"Presumed dead."

"Not presumed. She's dead," I lie. They must believe she's dead and not a prisoner of war, since all POWs are considered traitors.

"Olga Markovich witnessed the accident, but she's dead too." I just made this up, but they have no way of checking my story now.

With his bloodless lips, sharp nose, and close-set eyes, Orlyev evokes the aspect of a rodent. But what's far more repulsive is his vanity. His hairline is receding as fast as the German army, but he has obviously spent some amount of time combing the remaining strands over his bald head in what I'm sure he considers an artful arrangement. Semenov, on the other hand, has the appearance of a slightly wizened cherub. Everything is round— his cheeks, his nose, his completely bald head that gleams pinkly. Scattered with purple veins, his scalp suggests a kind of vascular cartography of some unknown land.

"We understand that you were shot down in the Ukraine . . ." Orlyev's beady eyes narrow. He pauses, and Semenov cuts in.

"Perhaps you had some contact with the Schutzmannschaft?"

Luckily, at that moment, Bershanskaya arrives. "Pardon me, gentlemen. I do not mean to interrupt, but Comrade Baskova's plane is ready."

I go back and find Galya. She has to know about Tatyana. We have to start planning now, but we can't let anyone overhear us. It's broad daylight, so we aren't yet flying, but we will in a matter of hours. The only place we can truly have privacy is in the cockpit of our U-2.

"Follow me," I call, and begin walking toward our plane.

"Why? I want to sleep."

"Not now; I want to run a compass check."

"A compass check? We just did one yesterday. Our compass is fine."

"Just be quiet and follow me."

Galya seems to sense this is not about a compass check at all. We reach the plane and climb into our cockpits. I unfold a map. "You see the bridgeheads that Commander Bershanskaya marked?"

She looks over. "Yes."

With a trembling finger, I point to an area south and east of Smolensk. "You see that?"

"Yes. It's beyond the bridgeheads. What is it?"

"Tatyana," I whisper. "She's in a prison camp there."

"You're kidding. How do you know this?"

"Yuri."

"Yuri? How can that be?"

"You know when Bershanskaya called me into her office?" She nods. "He was there."

I quickly explain about the POW camp and how he recognized her. "If the Germans don't kill her, the NKVD will capture her. That's what they do. They'll capture her and send her to the gulag as a slave."

Galya looks down and clenches her fists. "I heard rumors of this. We can't let it happen to your sister."

"As soon as the bridgeheads are secure, four divisions of the Red Army will go in. Some will go to these camps to 'liberate' the prisoners. But it will be no liberation. Russian trucks will come in to take the prisoners back east to another kind of death. Believe me."

She looks up at me. "I do."

There's a fierce light in her eyes, and I know my cause has become Galya's completely.

She and I begin planning immediately. Our first step is to stash a rucksack with helmet, goggles, and a flight jacket, so when we rescue Tatyana she'll be dressed as a pilot or a navigator and not in a prison suit. We measure the cockpits. They're each made for one person only, but we'll squeeze her in somehow. *She's probably rail thin after all these months in a prison camp,* I think grimly.

A few hours later, Galya and I take off along with other U-2s being sent to defend the bridgeheads. We spend the majority of the next few days in the sky, chasing away the Germans trying to destroy these crucial targets. Some of the other pilots succumb to exhaustion, but thinking about Tatyana keeps me going. The sooner we dispel the Germans, the sooner I'll be able to leave and rescue her.

One morning, shortly after we land from a night's work,

Galya comes out of the chart room, where the navigators often gather, and calls out, "Want to do a compass check?"

I know immediately what she means and head back toward our plane.

She unfolds a map. Not a navigation chart, but a map showing a large complex. "This is the camp," she says quietly. "And take a look at this." She jabs her finger at a spot on the map. "It's the infirmary where Tatyana is."

My eyes widen in disbelief as I look up at her. "How did you get this?"

"Don't ask. I'm putting it back as soon I can. Look at it now and remember it."

"Where's your calculation board?"

"Right here." She reaches into the cockpit pouch behind her seat.

I begin sketching madly. "Don't try to copy the whole plan of the camp," she cautions me.

"I won't. Just this area."

What Galya did was terribly dangerous. The charts are not supposed to leave the chart room. The bridgehead charts, of which there are many, are kept under lock and key until needed. I'm not sure how she managed this. But I am grateful.

"When do you want to get her?" Galya asks. "I heard the Germans are evacuating their prison camps. She might not be there for much longer."

"Tonight," I say. "After our mission. Instead of coming back to the base, we'll head to the camp." I pause, suddenly realizing how much I'm asking of Galya. "Or I can go by myself. It's close enough that I can get there without a navigator."

"You're not going anywhere without me," Galya says. "I'm in. Tonight it is."

# CHAPTER 24

As Galya and I taxi down the field, I feel a mixture of excitement and dread. I'm going to find my sister, but if we're caught, all three of us could be executed as traitors—me, Tatyana, *and* Galya. Talk about being caught between the devil and the deep blue sea—a favorite expression of my mother's. But there is no sea, just sky, and it's not blue. A fog is thickening. I just thank God that Galya is my navigator, my human calculator, which makes her almost as powerful as Superman with his X-ray vision. We, Galya and I, are the designated first-strike plane. Like the canary in the coal mine, we see how low we can dive with the first bomb load without getting knocked out by the blowback. If it works, Bershanskaya and two other pilots will swoop down.

There's no radio communication between our U-2s, only intercoms between pilot and navigator. Galya's voice crackles through the earphones. "Hello, Skipper," she says calmly. "Point five kilometers to target. Wind speed fifteen kilometers per hour. South by southeast. Holding heading two forty to maintain course. Altimeter twelve hundred meters, beginning descent now . . . Point two, take her down, Skipper."

I throttle back and begin a long, slow glide. How far will we dive? When will the canary breathe the poison? It won't be deadly fumes, just a terrible shuddering as the air convulses around us, shattering our fragile plane, ripping our chute packs from our backs, tearing our limbs from our bodies. My hand is sweaty on the stick as I keep pushing it forward. The nose tips down farther. My eyes are on the altimeter. We are grazing the six-hundred-meter limit. "Bomb latches disengaged, Skipper."

"Copy, Galya."

"Speed, Skipper?"

"Throttling back to cruise speed, sixty knots."

"Marked!" Galya says calmly. And I can feel the lurch as she releases the bombs. I pull back on the throttle and head straight up, accelerating to max speed. The plane shudders. There are many names for this shuddering blowback from bombing raids—some call it the devil's throat, or the maw of the winds, but we Night Witches call it the cat's cradle. But so far there are still wings on the plane. The propeller is still spinning, ailerons intact. Fifteen seconds later there is another shuddering explosion.

"Geronimo!" Galya yells. Bershanskaya must have made her hit. When I look down I see a carpet of flames engulfing the landscape. "We did it! We did it! Look, there's

Bershanskaya's plane. She made it! Made it out of the cat's cradle."

*Almost*, I think, for just as Bershanskaya's plane dissolves into a fog bank, I see something off to the port side.

"Jesus Christ!" Galya swears.

A German fighter plane has just emerged from the same fog. Probably missed Bershanskaya completely, but it had us in its sights. It's a Focke-Wulf, flying right at us. The nose of the plane lights up as he fires. I dive and then bank into a steep slide slip. I can still hear him firing. Tracer bullets like hail ping off our fuselage as we are pummeled. I cut the speed. He overshoots us. I see the swastika smeared across the night. But then my breath locks.

"He's coming back!" Galya's shouts nearly blast my ears off. I can see the Focke-Wulf coming confidently toward us. He owns the space and he knows it. My mind races desperately for a plan. Our only weapon is slowness. The tortoise must win this race. I work the rudder pedals madly to tip the craft this way and that to throw off his aim. He overshoots us again.

I feel Galya shift behind me. She's on her knees getting ready to fire the machine gun. With rear-mounted guns it limits our range. Can't shoot forward, only back or sideways. We're still a sitting duck. I push on the rudder pedal, begin to decelerate, then go for full rudder. "We're cartwheeling!" I shout. "Fire when we come up."

"Ready, Skipper." I hear the *chak chak chak* of the machine-gun fire. As the Focke-Wulf flashes by, I can see the pilot. He actually salutes me. But he's in no position to fire.

"Outta ammunition?" Galya gasps.

No such luck; he performs a steep banking turn and comes up under us. But I quickly peel away and plunge beneath him. It's the same maneuver I did in the Yak-7 that I flew to the temporary airbase. The German pilot fires but it's too late. He's far above us. We hear the bullets tattooing the nothingness of the night sky.

"Shoot the moon! Nazi bastard!" Galya fumes.

"How many rounds do those Folke-Wulf artillery guns carry?"

"Not sure, Skipper. But he might be coming back."

Everything seems so quiet now after the explosions of the ammo depot and the strafing from the Focke-Wulf. It's somewhat miraculous that although we were peppered with bullets, no serious damage was done.

"He's not going to go where we're going." I made the decision when I came out of the last loop. The conditions are perfect. The moon is just winking out as a cloud cover comes in. It's my favorite type of fog—layered. One sees this kind of layering in the mountains or sometimes by the sea, a strata of clear air between layers of fog. A fog sandwich. And we are cozy as butter between two slices of bread.

It's time for us to find my sister.

Galya guides us in the right direction. The layers of fog dissolve, revealing the stars. I gasp. There they are again: Alnitak, Alnilam, and Mintaka, burnishing the belt of Orion. *She's near,* I think. *She's near!*

I climb up and at twelve hundred meters begin a banking turn.

"The POW camp is up there on the left. Are you ready to go in?" Galya asks.

My heart is beating so fast, I can barely speak, but manage a faint "yes."

Tatyana shivered in the snow. It was just a matter of time before she would be shot. She knew it. Either the Germans would recapture her and shoot her on sight, or her own forces would capture her and execute her as a traitor. She braced for shouts, but there was just the howl of the wind. The entire world seemed to have been bleached into nothingness. She was uncertain if she was right side up or upside down in this ditch. But if she just stayed she would freeze to death. She had to move.

She began to scrabble her way out on her hands and knees. Crawling forward, she wiped the snow from her face. Her fingers touched the pit where her right eye had been before she had crashed those long months ago. The last thing she wanted to do was to catch up with the Nazis who had imprisoned her. Was she free of them at last?

The order for evacuation had come shortly before the Red Army's bombardment of the nearby ammunition depot. With the Russians coming nearer, German high command ordered that the camp near Elbing on the Vistula Lagoon be evacuated. The evacuation started ten hours before the bombardment began. The sound was deafening. Tatyana had wondered if the Night Bombers were part of this offensive. It would have been just their kind of mission. Five hundred or more of the prisoners, many Russians, Jews, and Roma people, had been staggering along rutted roads for hours. Several had died along the way. Several had been shot trying to escape. But as the Germans grew more frantic and weather worsened, Tatyana had found the perfect moment to run. And that's just what she did. She ducked out of the line of prisoners and sprinted for her life.

Tatyana blessed the whiteness of the snowy night, the complete silence. Still with no stars to guide her and only one eye to see them if they were there, she had to figure out which way was east, which direction would take her back to the Motherland and to her sister. She felt an unusual calmness steal over her as she gradually realized that she was in fact alone—completely alone for the first time since her capture. There was always noise in the camps: the barking of the guards, the announcements over the bullhorns, the *Aufseherinnen*, the matrons, stalking up and down the lineups, scowling, screaming orders, their crops raised ready to smack. They seemed to delight in smacking Tatyana near her pitted eye socket. She'd damaged her eye when she crashed, and the German doctors hadn't tried particularly hard to save it. There was hardly a day when it had not bled.

But now there was no blood. And there were no beatings, only this beautiful quiet world turned white with fog and silence. Perhaps this was death. It was so peaceful. *Yes, I have died.* All this time fearing death, but now it was here. *It's come for me,* just like in the poem by Emily Dickinson that she had so loved and won an award for in translation.

She sank to her knees, curling up to slip into the sublime slumber of that immortality. *My carriage is the white night, no haste I am at leisure.*

But something began to disturb this sweet passage, like a gnat, the annoying sibilance of a mosquito on a hot summer night. She forced her single eyelid open. *It can't be . . .* The sound was closer. It came like a soft hum now. She sat up. Her carriage had disappeared. The whiteness was gone. She looked up and saw three stars in Orion's Belt, and just beneath the tip of his sword, she could see in a shaft of bright moonlight a small aircraft. The hum of its engine purred in the night. It could only be a U-2.

Tatyana couldn't believe it. She jumped up and began waving her arms. The shaft of moonlight striped the ground. She ran toward it, flailing her arms, kicking up snow like small geysers. The antic shadows of her wild frolic sprinted across the band of moonlight.

"Look," Galya says over the microphone. "There's a long line of people marching. It must be the prisoners they're evacuating."

She's right. I squint, but the people are too far away to see distinctly. It's impossible to count the number of guards. I blink, then catch sight of something moving below, trailing behind the others by half a mile or so. My heart stops. "Galya, I knew it! I knew it. Look, there's a person down there. It's her. It's Tatyana."

"I see a shadow, but how do you know it's Tatyana?"

"I just do. Trust me."

"But how can we land? There's snow down there. It looks deep."

"It's not so deep where she is. It must be a road. Get ready. We'll make one pass to warn her and then we'll land." I glance at the fuel gauge. "Correct that. We're landing now. Not enough fuel to make a pass. Just enough to get back to base with this tailwind."

I start a banking turn and head into the wind. Easing back on the throttle, I cut my speed to barely above stalling. I feel us touch down, and then we stop abruptly. The snow is deep. No matter; I'll think about takeoff later.

The gaunt figure begins walking toward us as I climb out of the cockpit.

"Valya!" The sound scratches the air. But it's not just a

sound in this long night of an endless war. It is my name. My sister is calling my name.

"Tatyana!"

We both break into a run and fall into each other's arms. She is shaking violently, though I'm not sure if it's from cold or crying. I can feel her sharp bones under her ragged cloak. I tear off my flight jacket and stuff her into it. We embrace again. I can feel her tears and mine mingling as we press our faces together. But I also feel something else. There is something different about her face as it presses against mine. I draw my head back, stunned by what I see, or don't see.

"I lost it in the crash," Tatyana says, trembling. "But it could have been worse."

"Worse? You mean you could have died."

"Yes, that." She smiles crookedly.

"Quick, let's get you into the plane," Galya says. "Then we'll have to clear something for a runway. This snow is deep."

We help Tatyana into the rear cockpit, giving her our chocolate bars to eat while Galya and I go to clear the snow. We have to clear off two hundred meters of it in order to be able to take off.

I look at Galya and mutter, "It's a lot of snow. How are we going to do this?" But Galya is not looking at me, but the plane. She has what I call "that look." She is calculating.

"Your sister probably doesn't weigh more than, what? Thirty-five kilos?"

"You're thinking about fuel, right?"

"Not just fuel. Look at our bomb racks."

"What about them?"

"They're not *just* bomb racks."

"Huh? What are they if they aren't just bomb racks?"

"You think we can just scuff this snow away and clear two hundred meters for takeoff with our hands and feet? We can use the racks as snowplows. Or scrapers." My eyes widen. I look at the frame of the bomb racks. They are perfect for scraping off snow.

Galya runs for the toolbox and together we start dismantling the racks.

Once we start pushing the snow aside, we realize that the footsteps of the retreating prisoners have packed down most of it, so our work is a little easier. Tatyana tries to help but we won't let her. It takes us close to an hour to clear the new snow. By the time we climb back in the plane, Tatyana is curled up sleeping in the rear cockpit. I stare at her face. The scar boils up diagonally across the left side of her face. She opens her right eye and looks at me.

"Shrapnel," she says quietly. "Do I scare you?"

"Never!" I lean over my seat and kiss her forehead. Galya and Tatyana are squashed in the rear cockpit. The weight seems fine as we taxi, and a minute later we are lifting off into a clear starry night. The fuel gauge is hovering barely above empty. I think our approach glide is done on fumes.

But we make it.

# CHAPTER 25

Commander Yevdokiya Bershanskaya sways slightly as she stands by her desk, staring at us in disbelief. Tatyana is propped up between Galya and me. If she weighs thirty kilos, I would be surprised.

"What is this?" she whispers.

"Tatyana Petrovna Baskova, reporting for duty." Tatyana makes a sound halfway between a gasp and a chuckle.

Bershanskaya comes out from behind her desk and folds Tatyana into her arms, then leads her to a chair.

"Sit down, the three of you." I can almost see the gears of her brain working behind the intense green eyes. "This is going to be our story. We found you not today but months ago, staggering east, toward the Urals, as all good Russian soldiers are supposed to do in order to evade capture by the Nazis. You had been hiding out all the time, surviving in the woods, stealing from farms, whatever. We need not get too detailed. Serafima Krutosky and her navigator, Elena Pashuka, picked you up."

"But they're dead," I say.

"That's the point," Bershanskaya says evenly. "I'll alter the records."

"But . . . but . . . ," Tatyana begins to stammer. "But what about the others?"

"The other Night Bombers?" Tatyana nods. "Is that what you want to know? Will they rat you out? Never! They are steadfast. You see, one of the things that bind us is this dirty little secret—the NKVD and SMERSH. But now we have a sweet little secret to protect. And that is you."

The sweet secret is kept. A week later Tatyana climbs back in a U-2 and takes her first flight. A few months after that, she is leading a squadron. We're flying raids in east Prussia, supporting the allied American and British forces who had started the bombing of Berlin in February. On April 30, Hitler commits suicide in a bunker fifty-five feet beneath the chancellery in Berlin.

The war ends officially on May 8, 1945. We are at an American airbase when it happens. But for many Russians, the war does not really end. Or rather a new one begins. The Yalta Conference in February had a provision requiring that all prisoners of war and displaced persons be returned to their home countries, whether they wanted to go or not. For many Soviets it meant imprisonment or death.

But we return. Tatyana and I and the rest of the Night Witches fly our tiny planes east in early June. And we come back as heroes.

It is a bright autumn day as we stand in a line in Red Square. I am between Tatyana and Galya. We are three among twenty-four of the 588th Night Bombers Regiment who are about to be awarded the Hero of the Soviet Union medal by the general secretary of the Central Committee of the Communist Party of the Soviet Union. We should just call him *murderer.* I am trembling as Joseph Vissarionovich Stalin pins the medal on me. It is simple compared with some: A plain gold star suspended from a small swatch of red cloth.

"Ah, I can almost feel your heart beating, my dear." His thick lips spread into an avuncular smile. His heavy black eyebrows dance up toward his hairline, and he actually gives my cheek a little pinch. "You won't wash your face now, eh?" he jokes. But I see the flash of something unspeakably brutal in the blackness of his eyes. He moves on toward Tatyana.

"The Motherland is eternally grateful for your valor and courage." I see her swallow and look down. She sometimes has nightmares that Stalin has discovered she was a POW.

An hour later Tatyana and I return to our little government-provided attic apartment. We now live in Moscow. We sit down and I fix us each a mug of tea. Our medals are on the table between us. "What are we supposed to do with these things?" Tatyana mutters.

"Hang them up. Display them. We are heroes of the Soviet Union." She catches the edge in my voice.

She shakes her head. "But what about the POWs who fought as hard and are now in Stalin's prison camps? The gulag." We both look at each other. The words do not need to be spoken. We both know. As long as there is a gulag, we cannot display these medals. I get up and go to a drawer and fetch a napkin. We fold the medals carefully in the cloth. Tatyana takes them back to a drawer and shuts it.

"Someday, perhaps," she whispers.

"Someday," I repeat.

We stay up late, very late, as we cannot sleep. Sleeping has come hard for us since the war. I reach across the narrow space to Tatyana's bed and shake her shoulder.

"You awake?"

"Of course."

"Let's go to the roof."

There's a door in the ceiling with a sliding ladder that leads onto the roof of our apartment. We often go up there at night to look at the stars and visit the constellations that we know so well from over one thousand nights of flying. We let the darkness fold around us. Like a quilt, it gathers us into the downy beauty of the night.

"Are you sure you want to go up now?" Tatyana asks. "It's too late for stars. It's almost dawn."

"Yes, let's go see the sky anyway, see the dawn."

We start up the ladder. As Tatyana and I climb out through the trapdoor to the roof, the sky is just turning pink.

Tatyana sighs. "We never really saw the dawn when we were witches, did we?"

"Not once that I can remember." But I do recall hating the dawn the morning that Mama was killed, wanting to curse it and wondering how the sun dared to rise. However, now, as the dawn breaks, a calmness steals over me. I take Tatyana's hand. I no longer resent the sun, but I do feel that this dawn seems a bit forlorn. There's an emptiness in the world, as if not enough people can marvel at the colors that bloom so quietly in the sky on this morning.

"Look!" Tatyana exclaims softly, and points toward the horizon.

"What?"

"A shadow of the moon. A daylight moon."

The blanched sphere hovers like a ghost in the sky, with no trace of its silvery nighttime countenance.

We watch as the two orbs float just above the horizon, one a dusky shadow of its nighttime silver, the other growing bolder and brighter with each moment. Two sibling spheres rising. Tatyana and I marvel at the spectacle. I grasp her hand tighter. We have each other. We are not heroes. We are sisters. Sisters forever.

# ACKNOWLEDGMENTS

I am deeply indebted to two people—two navigators, if you will, who kept me true to course. First is Tom Ricks, Senior Advisor on National Security at The New America Foundation, and a former Washington Post Pulitzer prize-winning Pentagon correspondent. His knowledge of World War II was invaluable, and he pointed me in the direction of so many vital troves for my research. I am also endlessly appreciative of my gifted editor, Mallory Kass, who has guided my craft skillfully through so many books. I am blessed by these two friendships.

# ABOUT THE AUTHOR

Kathryn Lasky is the author of over fifty books for children and young adults, including the Guardians of Ga'Hoole series, which has more than seven million copies in print, and was turned into a major motion picture, *Legend of the Guardians: The Owls of Ga'Hoole*. Her books have received numerous awards including a Newbery Honor, a Boston Globe-Horn Book Award, and a Washington Post-Children's Book Guild Nonfiction Award. She lives with her husband in Cambridge, MA.